Plenty of Carp:

A Fishing Guide for Dating Singles

Plenty of Carp:

A Fishing Guide for Dating Singles

CINDY LUCY

iUniverse, Inc.
Bloomington

Plenty of Carp
A Fishing Guide for Dating Singles

iUniverse books may be ordered through booksellers or by contacting:

iUniverse
1663 Liberty Drive
Bloomington, IN 47403
www.iuniverse.com
1-800-Authors (1-800-288-4677)

ISBN: 978-1-4502-8307-6 (sc)
ISBN: 978-1-4502-8306-9 (ebook)
ISBN: 978-1-4502-8305-2 (dj)

Printed in the United States of America

iUniverse rev. date: 2/28/2011

To Roger

The best laid plans of mice and men.

—*Robert Burns*

Preface

My one and only husband died in 2004. The first two years after his death were emotionally crippling, and it wasn't until year three that I could actually entertain the thought of dating another man. My journey to find Mr. Right has been a fishing trip on many lakes only to find Carp (in the plural form, just like sheep, moose, and deer). I refer to these men as "*Uno mas no mas.*" This is Spanish for "one more, no more," and this means that after meeting a Carp once, I choose not to meet him or his flapping lips and tail again. A second meeting only adds insult to injury, so why bother with *dos mas* when there are so many Carp swimming in the murky waters?

I first became interested in writing about my dating experiences after having no success with the dating/fishing scene. I used multiple online and commercial dating sources, which only resulted in landing multiple Carp. As an older fishing gal, each Fish presented himself with multiple bags, and all of it was free without my asking. I have sat across from men who told me stories even they could not make up. I also interviewed gals from their early twenties to the wonderful age of the seventies, who assured me my fishing stories were universal, in that they happen to all gals regardless of age. With tales from the Carps' lips, I decided to capture these moments with humor. Of course, they are embellished with soap opera drama and bubbles (or maybe it is the *Phantom of the Opera* drama). They are my journey and history of the fishing scene.

To set the record straight, I enjoyed meeting all of my Carp. For without those first-time dates, I could not have written this book and shared my fishing stories with all of you. My hope is that you will be able to relate to one of these short stories or poems; I will be thrilled if you can relate to more than one. Relating is the intent, since all of the stories had one key element fueling my mania. Andy Warhol said it best when he said, "Everyone will be famous for fifteen minutes." If you find yourself in this book, feel flattered that I took the time to give you fifteen minutes of fame. You could have gone through life without recognition and remained anonymous. The next step may be a Broadway play or film. If Jack Nicholson can appear in a hospital gown with his backside to the audience, then there is hope Carp may be cast with rubbery lips, flapping tails, and their backsides too. This is my gift to all of you, my present for a little slice of your life.

Acknowledgments

Lovingly, to Robin who read my final manuscript and laughed out loud and keeping the reasons for laughter a secret from my son. With smiles to Dr. Patti Cakes P., who reviewed and critiqued with tender loving care all of my short stories and poems and helped me to find my voice. With smiles, to Cindy B., who laughed at my life and was amazed that I could accomplish so much in a week let alone twenty-four hours. To wine and dine Susie Q., who honored and welcomed my effort by making a video accompanying this book. Lastly, I acknowledge all who supported an endeavor many have always dreamed of doing and used me as their instrument of voice and providing peace of mind that we are not always dealt a deck of cards but in many instances a bucket of Carp.

Contents

Introduction

The charm of fishing is that it is the pursuit of what is elusive
but attainable, a perpetual series of occasions for hope.

—*John Buchan, The Thirty-Nine Steps and Greenmantle*

This book includes short stories, poems, and quotes from the perspective of an older gal. I have interviewed women as young as nineteen to women in their seventies; they all agreed that Carp stories are ageless. Interviews with men confirm that they can be Carp. One fella told me they are animals. Both genders agreed that dating experiences were laughable and should not be taken seriously if one wants to continue fishing for the so-called "Big One."

The format for the Carp short stories specifically follows an online dating profile married with the essence of the five-paragraph essay. First, each selection is introduced with an Incoming Carp E-mail advertising his positive characteristics as a lure. Second, as a lover of other people's wisdom, a Carp Quote is used as a fishing line further enhancing the Carp's attributes or casting a specific light with regard to the content of the experience. Third, the Carp Skeleton, or the Preface, provides background or historical information giving the reader a frame of reference. Fourth, the Carp Flesh, or the Novella, is the actual short story. Lastly, the Carp Tail, or the Epilogue, provides closure, a summary, and may provide direction or advice. These are the 1970's Jack Nicolson's *Five Easy Pieces* complementing a five-paragraph essay. Creative license and 2011 provides the "sixth easy piece" courtesy of

Cindy Lucy which is a final quote breaking the net and releasing the Carp into the murky waters of bottom feeders.

As a life-time lover of kids and teaching, I have referenced my past with regard to education, more specifically math. I have learned most problems in life can be solved with simple basic facts, sense, and reasoning. In addition, after being alive for a very long time, my brain has trapped connections to television, music, and movies. My mind is a kaleidoscope of impressions made from the business of entertainment. Bee, my long time friend, once said to me, "How can you stand living in that head? Your mind is an iron trap." I think I was in my late twenties at the time. Due to time, I have cross-referenced these connections for both the young and the getting older. My hope is that you will enjoy my journey with fishing and understand the choice with regard to tackle from the box.

Fishing with Carp means going through a lot of Crap.

Airports and Airplanes
Angel Fish

The best looking men
are in the airport,
and on airplanes.

When meeting
we become locked
in a time warp
with no past
and no future.

Our time together is
about the present
and being present.

Eyes observe
Adidas logo wear
trim, fit build
business attaché
just the right height
pleasant face with smile
genuinely interested.

All is wonderful when
meeting in an airport
nothing to do
but pass the time
no past, no future,
just a twilight zone
in a fifth dimension.

Cindy Lucy

Boarding planes
couples part
no past, no future
only the present
the gift is gone.

One goes to London
on business
one goes home
to other business
a memory.

Part I
Elementary School:
Beginning Fishing

*Everyone has to start somewhere and that
is why it is called the beginning.*

—Cindy Lucy

*Nothing grieves a child more to study the wrong
lesson and learn something he wasn't suppose to.*

—E. C. McKenzie

Peas and Carrots

Incoming Carp E-mail: I am a fabulous companion on holidays and known for my charming personality, washboard six-pack stomach muscles, stalking, and spending time sorting peas and carrots. My passion is writing pornographic novels.

My brain is my second favorite organ.

—*Woody Allen*

Introduction: How can something that looks and feels so good hurt so much? I am past the pain but must admit this particular Carp left me wounded and crippled for some time. "Once bitten, twice shy babe" is not only true with Ian Hunter and rock and roll but also resonated with this particular Carp. The more contemporary summation of what Peas and Carrots did to me can be found in the lyrics sung by Lady Gaga: "He ate my heart and then he ate my brain." Due to his dishonest behavior, Peas and Carrots is now in my "no memory" folder.

The Novella: For the most part, Peas and Carrots did not appear to be the type to hide in a closet and sort vegetables. I met him on a beach vacation, and what happens on the beach, stays on the beach. I did not know our meeting was going to be as hard as Nine Inch Nails, due to my thinking that beach vacations become real-life relationships.

Meeting Peas and Carrots, who is no relation to Forrest Gump, was surreal and magical. The week was filled with smiles and the feeling of warmth coming from the depths of my womanly parts. It was a feat for me to even walk to the beach without convulsing with spasms of delight. Everything was glorious, and the end of vacation was nowhere in sight. We walked into this adventure with our *Eyes Wide Shut*. Even though I was able to make a connection to the movie with Tom Cruise and Nicole Kidman, I would have made the same mistake. If big-time movie stars have *Eyes Wide Shut*, then the rest of the regular population should also be included.

Peas and Carrots and I had our *Eyes Wide Shut* regularly, since we kept bumping into each other. He would be returning from a golf game and see me on the beach, and we would mostly just look at each other. In passing, he commented that I looked nice in a bikini, slathered in suntan oil. Then there was the nightly visit to the beach bar, which included tequila shots. I never had a shot of tequila before, and I have no idea why I waited so long. One shot of tequila equals forty-five minutes of nonstop laughter. There is no better way to spend a vacation than yucking it up. Two shots of tequila guarantee success, with more yucking. Three shots of tequila guarantee up-chucking with no yucking, unless you count dry heaves as the prerequisite laughter. So I stuck with two shots. We had a daily and nightly routine of sunning, yucking, and bumping into each other, thus "Are you stalking me?" became our personal joke. This, of course, is only while vacationing; it should be a Dating Rule: Keep your *Eyes Wide Shut* while on vacation, but remember your eyes must be wide open when you return to the real world.

The first mistake with Peas and Carrots was not realizing that he was only out of the closet and not sorting vegetables when he was on vacation. He was charming and affectionate, said wonderful things, and made me feel like I could love him for the rest of my life. I loved that feeling of butterflies in my stomach. It had been so long since the last time, I thought my butterflies had been netted and stick-pinned within a frame for display. We smiled, spent time in the sun, and walked hand-in-hand for the better parts of the day. There were even better times at night, and they did not involve sorting vegetables. I wish these adventures could be bottled and put on a shelf in the pantry. Then when it is cold, miserable, and lonely, I would just have to pick up this jar, open the lid, and experience all of the warmth all over again. I wonder if I can find this deal on e-Bay.

Vacations are whirlwinds. Before they begin, they come to an end. Peas and Carrots shared his e-mail address, even though he lived a couple of thousand miles away. What is a couple of thousand miles when there is warmth in the loins? Warmth has driven couples crazy mad, and this energy allows them to conquer anything in leaps and bounds. Peas and Carrots became my vision of Superman and I would be his Lois Lane. Science fiction is something I am able to completely accept.

Alas, this first was also to be my last with Peas and Carrots. Learning was a curve with this particular species, and mistakes may make me smarter. The operative word is "may." With Carp, I just didn't know if smarter was a variable that solved the equation with matters of the heart. With many miles between us, Peas and Carrots added my notch to his belt, and he wasn't even Mexican. Hopefully, Mexican men are not insulted since my intent is pure. I learned from a Mexican soap opera that notches on a belt are the marks of the number of female conquests. Referencing this connection to Peas and Carrots, who incidentally is not Mexican but a Carp, made the point I was a conquest and not to be considered seriously.

Once Peas and Carrots had completed his holiday, he returned to his closet to count his notches and resume cleaning closets and sorting vegetables. Maybe he was flossing his teeth with his belt since the gaps between them were large enough to emit deadly lies. He only acknowledged a few e-mails and did not return my phone calls. Once the holiday was over, so was Peas and Carrots. This is what I thought.

I spoke with Peas and Carrots' good traveling friend, who was also on the same holiday; I will refer to him as Lover Boy. This reference is not due to indiscretions but because he is genuine and so easy to love. Lover Boy explained that Peas and Carrots would be cleaning closets and sorting vegetables for quite some time. His past was full of run-ins with the local police due to his indiscretions. His offenses involved publishing advertisements in the local Buyer's Guide, advertising himself as a "prime fillet-o-fish sandwich," using this tactic as a front for finding available women and producing offspring. The sandwich ad had women drooling at his door. Once inside the Castle of Fish, which is the name of his establishment, his victims lose control of their womanly parts, and like the parting of the Red Sea, Peas and Carrots parts their most important part. Thus, he has impregnated dozens of women, producing numerous children, but has never married. After learning this information, I was certainly glad I had already been through menopause.

Lover Boy continued to tell me that Peas and Carrots was a real piece of work (and he was not referring to art). It seemed he was very confused with who he was sexually and relied on sorting peas and carrots to figure out his sexual tendencies for the day. *Dazed and Confused* (and with no help from Matthew McConaughey), he finds himself in the closet trying to figure out who he is. Armed with a bag of frozen peas and carrots, he opens the bag and separates the peas from the carrots. If peas win the number count, then he chases women for the day. If carrots win, then he chases men for the day. I wonder what would happen if there were a tie in the number of peas and carrots. I guess he would have both sexual preferences and just keep track by saying, "Eenie meenie miney mo." With this information from Lover Boy, I now understood it must have been peas the day he met me. Funny, I never saw any carrot fellas on the in-between days.

Peas and Carrots would leave the country several times a year due to his closet phobia and mania for sorting vegetables. It seemed he had become notorious and had been compared to the likes of Baby Face Nelson, since both of them are cleaner-uppers of sorts. Baby Face Nelson cleaned banks, while Peas and Carrots cleaned women's uteruses with his spermacide, formaldehyde, or maybe it is pesticide. Any Carp making it a practice to create litters with no consciousness or restitution is stinky chum.

Before Peas and Carrots decided to do another sorting of the vegetables, he communicated with me by writing a very long pornographic letter. At first, I mistook this for a love note, since he detailed multiple acrobatic acts, describing all his body parts with appropriate adjectives. I believe Woody Allen equated this with the most important male organ, which comes first before the brain. His note was a detailed description of multiple uses of a swinging thing and his balls, and I am not referring to the kind that makes baskets, drop into holes, or goes rolling down the alley.

At first, I was shocked, repulsed, and emotionally hurt that he would show such lack of thought for my feelings and how I would respond. After the second and third read, I decided he had a lot of passion for his balls. Peas are tiny balls, so he must have been fixated with round shapes. Also, I have learned that the things we are the closest to become our expressions of passion, but in Peas and Carrots' case, his balls became delusions of grandeur.

I think the intent of his letter was to morally shock me; maybe he hoped I would send it to *Adam and Eve* for publication. In reality, he may be a starving writer desiring to be a part of the lucrative world of pornographic publications. He also may have lots of palimony bills, since he chose to be a so-called "pal" to lots of children. I am not sure any of them refer to him as Papa. Maybe the ones he shared peas and carrots with would consider referencing him with this name since he made sure they ate healthy from one of the four food groups. Whatever; I have nothing else profound to say at this time (or ever) with regard to a guy who goes by the name of Peas and Carrots.

Lover Boy has been my e-mail friend for the past several years. He is no longer friends with Peas and Carrots, nor will he be doing future travels with him. Lover Boy calls him "psycho vegetable." He doesn't know from one day to the next whether he will be a pea or a carrot and considers him a pea brain and next in line for life as a chicken. Bestowed as chicken, he no longer will sort peas and carrots but will be poking his beak around in a fenced-in area scavenging bits of corn. I wonder what sexual preference corn is.

An update from Lover Boy tells me Peas and Carrots admitted himself to the Institute of Sexual Anomalies and agreed to let the staff use his mind for research. The goal of Project Corn is to gather data with regard to corn and the sexual tendencies when compared to the control groups of peas and carrots. The only time he is allowed off the premises is for his daily visit to the optometrist and the health club hot tub. The optometrist is necessary since his vision has become impaired due to counting peas and carrots in the dark recesses of his closet. The hot tub is physical therapy. Warm balls fire blanks, and this keeps him safe from the female population. He is allowed to chase them but not to catch and impregnate. The same goes for the fella carrots (but impregnation is not an issue).

Lover Boy chooses not to associate with Peas and Carrots any longer since he is truly a whole lot of ass instead of just being an asshole, which is much smaller in comparison. Also, Peas and Carrots blamed Lover

Boy for some of the offspring, and this is unconscionable. To this day, he chooses not to eat mixed vegetables.

This holiday with Peas and Carrots was nice on the surface, but in reality it was really quite scary. My eyes were definitely wide shut then, but they are wide open now. Today, I find it hard to believe I could be so enamored with such a Carp. With regard to the Kingdom of Carp, I have to count him below zero on the number line, which qualifies him as "feces." He certainly is below chum.

Epilogue: Lover Boy heard from Peas and Carrots that he had been dismissed from the Institute of Sexual Anomalies. The data accumulated from Project Corn indicated that he was schizophrenic and not a reliable source for study since he confused corn with chick peas. *Harold and His Purple Crayon* may be back to the drawing board, but Peas and Carrots is back to sorting round and square frozen vegetables.

> *It's bizarre that the produce manager is more important to my children's health than the pediatrician.*
>
> —*Meryl Streep*

Getting Ready for Fishing

Getting ready for fishing
is always fun for me.
I love to play dress up,
actually do dress up,
and totally am about dress up
is not an effort for me.

Getting ready for fishing
love the squeaky clean,
trendy clothing,
makeup and accessories,
first impressions are a must be.

Getting ready for fishing
in general may be in vain.
For the meeting on the dock
may deliver a Carp without a brain.

Two hours to get ready
and what does it bring,
Carp of every species
who do not maintain.

There are Carp with nose hairs, ear hairs,
and those who have more hair
sprouting from the top of their shirts.

There are Carp with wide bellies,
handlebar bellies, short bellies, and
jelly in their bellies.

There are Carp with no butts,
saggy butts,
and wear pants that reveal butts.

Cindy Lucy

There are Carp with some teeth,
very few teeth,
and yellow teeth with matching eyes.

Although
getting ready for fishing is still fun for me
regardless of what the fishing brings, you see
it may be the best two hours I spent on me
and for that, I smile happily.

Dancing with Woodcock

Incoming Carp E-mail: Looking for anyone who does not wear glasses and does not like to dance. Gals responding must be able to listen to unsavory conversation including bouts of diarrhea, jail house rock, and travels with lost luggage.

> *This is my dance space. This is your dance space. I*
> *don't go into yours, you don't go into mine.*
> —*Patrick Swayze (Johnny Lee),* Dirty Dancing, *1987*

Introduction: Four years ago, I met two single gals from Nebraska in Puerto Vallarta, Mexico. I was shocked to learn they were from Nebraska, since I thought the state was owned and operated by corn manufacturers and the only inhabitants were cows. Needless to say, we had a great week together and decided to spend another week in the summer at my house as a gals' week of single fun. I considered myself newly single, and they had been single for several years. They helped me to feel better about my single self and with being comfortable around single men.

The Novella: During this week of vacation, I entertained the gals by taking them to singles clubs, dances, festivals, and other sites in Michigan. This was not a difficult charge, and even Kid Rock knows best with references from his song, "Summertime in Northern Michigan." The lyrics closest to my Michigan heart include "splashing on the sandbar, talking by the campfire, catching walleye by the dock, and watching waves roll off the rocks." With all these exciting things on the agenda, I also understood they had to include meeting single men.

The first few nights the Ya Yas (my nickname for my corn-on-the-cob sisters) spent in Michigan were just that: nights. We stopped at the Lake Pub Karaoke Bar, took a drive to Lake Michigan, and ate dinner at a bar and grill. None of these events elicited single men. I next mentioned the Saturday Night Singles Dance, and the Ya Yas chorused "Alleluia" (and attending church wasn't even a part of the agenda). They agreed it would be fun to get dressed up and strut on the dance floor. At my age, the closest comparison would be to a cougar, and I have never seen a cougar strut. I guess my stance is to prowl and snarl. At fifty-plus years, most of the men would probably be much younger than me, and the ones who weren't were probably just terribly old, couldn't dance, and were just looking for younger gals as a substitute for a big plasma TV. So if some of them were grazing, I'd just take a look at what brings the steers out of their corrals or the Fish out of their schools.

Getting ready for the dance caused a problem. Within a matter of minutes, we blew a fuse due to everyone using blow dryers. I checked all the breakers and could not find the problem. I had no idea where to get an electrician on a Saturday night, so I called a neighbor. Luckily, he had a business card from one in the area. The fella arrived shortly and began throwing switches. He flipped the magic switch, and holy mackerel, I had electricity. I was dumbfounded, since I had done the same thing. He told me the switch was sticky and I had to pull it back hard, otherwise it would not budge. Well, this was a nice way to spend sixty-five dollars. He also told me only one gal at a time should blow dry her hair, otherwise he may be making another service call. This little episode put our agenda back about forty-five minutes. Oh well, what the hell. Gals have to have dry hair to go anywhere. It really wouldn't have mattered to me either way. It was summer in western Michigan, and wet hair would have been fine.

So with dry hair, I looked in my closet for something to wear on this hot summer night. My favorite noncolor is black, so black it is. I tried on a black layered peasant skirt, definitely not cougar material but closer to the panther look, and a matching black top that showed off my muscular arms. My sons have told me I have "guns." I never understood what this meant until I saw a picture of myself dancing with my son at his wedding. The picture was taken from the balcony from the side view. The side of my arms actually looked like a gun with the stock as the top part of my arm and the rest of the gun followed. It took me fifty-plus years to figure out I had guns.

For the most part, I have thought of my arms as chicken wings. This picture was fueled by my oldest son during my marathon-running days. He told me he could always pick me out in a race because he could see my arms flapping in the wind like chicken wings. To this day, I still struggle with the chicken that may be a part of me. Finally, it is time for me and my guns and my Ya Yas and their thirty-eights to head out to the local saloon that holds the singles dance.

Forty-five minutes and a cover charge of seven dollars later, we were looking at the dance floor. There were two rooms for dancing. One room was for ballroom dancing, and the other room was for dancing that required partners. I know you are thinking, all dancing involves a partner, but this room was for dancing of which you better know what you are doing. If you don't, you will be stepped on, pushed to the side, given looks that would raise the dead, and talked about to a neighbor. Can you imagine how mortifying it was for someone who just wanted to join in and have fun?

I am a pretty good dancer and a quick learner. In fact, one Fish from a vacation in Cabo San Lucas told me he loved my dancing since I was uninhibited and carefree without being downright naughty. In addition, I did not spend sixty-five dollars for the electrician and seven dollars to enter an outdated prom night to put up with high school snobbish behavior. The only cliques I planned to consider were the clicking of my fingers to the music. Does anyone click or snap their fingers any more? I think the Latin dancers do.

The Singles Dance was truly a picture belonging in a high school yearbook. As with high school, the Singles Dance was overrated. Both are just a snapshot of our lives that gets more play time than the movie *Gone with the Wind* (or for you youngsters, *High School Musical*). High school once, Singles Dance once, put the pictures in the drawer (or better yet, in the shredder). This is the behavior of the high school hop dancers who reside in the group dancing room. They are all playing the part of Scarlett O'Hara and Rhett Butler or Troy Bolton and Gabriella Montez.

Surprisingly, a Fish asked me to dance. He looked young and probably was. I looked younger and probably was not. I had no idea why the first thought that came into my head was age. Maybe it was because my mother told me when I was younger that women stopped aging at twenty-five. I was now older than twenty-five, so I must have two feet in the dirt (or maybe I am up to my hips).

I will refer to him as Quick Carp in this fishing episode. It does not take Quick Carp very long to cast a lure. He asked if I had other gal friends and if we would be willing to go to a friend's house in Saugatuck (a small town in good ole southern Michigan). Carp alert went off in my head, and I saw the word "fornicator" emblazoned on Quick Carp's forehead. It was time to go to the bathroom and take my piece of paper out of my bra for Plan B. I know this piece of paper will read, "Stay away from fornicators."

I did the right thing for a change and said, "Thanks, but no thanks. My Ya Yas are from Nebraska and they have to be back in the morning to pick corn."

The *Gone with the Wind* room had lost its flavor, much like salmon left unrefrigerated overnight; I decided to go to the room that was for freestyle dancing. This generally meant everyone just did their own thing, and no one cared what they looked like. People like to dance and just do it. On the west side of the floor was a bar that ran the entire length of the room. It was lined with barstools and men who were choosing not to dance. These fellas were the "grazers." Much like cows, they were mooing at what they saw on the dance floor. I decided to join the grazers.

This room, with mostly men, was not very crowded. The younger men were milling around close to the dance floor, grazing for lean meat. A little leg of lamb probably would be fine with them too. The men at the bar were older and did not appear to be too interested in getting up to dance; they were using the scene as a visual while chewing their cud. I should ask the Ya Yas if this made sense to them, since they are versed in cows and corn.

I decided to sit at the bar and drink a glass of wine. Restless, I got up and watched the few couples who were dancing. One gal was very tall, and her skirt had a slit all the way up to her "please look at my Saturday underwear." It was now apparent why the younger Fish were swimming so close to the dance floor. All the better to see if "Little Red Slit up the Dress" was inviting sharks for an after-dance snack. Carp are so easy to figure out. Show them a little skin, part of a boob, the back of a butt with a g-string or thong, and they pant, drool, blow bubbles, and become helpless. A gal could probably take the car keys out of a slippery Carp's back pocket and drive off with his vehicle before the bubbles burst in midair. So much for Grand Theft Auto.

After walking around a bit, I began a conversation with a skinny, baldheaded Fish. He was okay looking with a slight, athletic build; I will refer to him as Woodcock Carp because he reminded me of Mr. Woodcock from *Butch Cassidy and the Sundance Kid*. Woodcock was the skinny, stubborn Fish who would not give up the train's safe to Paul Newman and Robert Redford, the dynamic duo of bank robbers from the cowboy era.

Woodcock Carp and I talked for a while about nothing that I can remember, so it must have been nothing. He did tell me he could not dance. I wondered why he was at a dance when he didn't dance and talked about nothing. I decided this was a better situation than dancing with the fornicator (and also much safer). So we continued to talk about nothing and did not dance.

During our conversation of not getting to know one another, Mr. Woodcock Carp asked me to take off my glasses. This really took me aback, since I had never had anyone ask me to do this before. My late husband said I was one of a very few who could wear glasses and actually make it work, so I thought my glasses were a strong point.

I told Woodcock Carp, "No, I like my glasses and they are staying on my face. I have worn glasses since I was eleven years old, and I am not taking them off for a complete stranger. Also, I almost went blind when I was five years old due to a terrible bout of the measles. There was no vaccine at the time, and I spent most of kindergarten in my bedroom with the shades drawn. My glasses are my safety net."

Woodcock Carp continued to pester me to the point where I decided to walk away. He stopped me and said he was only interested in seeing the real color of my eyes. I still did not take off my glasses. I do understand today it was a fair question but was much too personal in nature with first-time fishing.

With what transpired so far at the Singles Dance, you may think this story is over, but it is not. Woodcock Carp decided to hold onto me for some reason. Maybe it was the excitement of fishing with a lure, fantasizing about my eye color, or maybe he enjoyed talking about nothing and not dancing. Regardless, he changed the subject and began telling me about his ex-wife. So, here it comes, the ex-wife and the rest of the story. I wonder if Paul Harvey enjoyed his work with the rest of the story.

For me, the rest of the story becomes a slippery slope of gloom, doom, blaming, and judging. Ex-wives, take note to see if this rings true for you. Use these as weapons by putting reminders on sticky notes inside your bra. They will make great Plan Bs when you go fishing and snag a Carp. Examples of Plan B notes may read, "My ex is incarcerated in a northern Michigan Corrections Institution for posing as a Walleye instead of a Carp. My ex is making a commercial for Depends, and depending on the sales, I plan to receive dividends as part of my financial settlement. My ex is in Omaha doing a sequel to *Up in the Air* with George Clooney and is playing the part of a corn husker. My ex left the country and so should you. X marks my spot so get off of mine." I am sure yours will be much more creative.

Epilogue: Cow and corn Ya Yas returned to Nebraska, singing with Kid Rock about "Summertime in Northern Michigan," and made it home in time to pick corn.

If dancing were any easier it would be called football.

—*Anonymous*

Regular Jail Carp—*"Now if You Know the Rest of the Story"*—Paul Harvey

Anyone who isn't confused really doesn't understand the situation.

—Edward R. Murrow

The rest of the story begins where the other story left off. For some reason, Mr. Woodcock Carp started talking about his ex-wife, and the conversation about nothing was over and a new one began. He told me Alexis, not her name but sounds like a good name for an ex, was married for seventeen years to an occupational prisoner. This means he was in and out of jail as a regular business. Alexis and Regular Jail Carp finally divorced. There was a suitcase involved, which is a little two-year-old girl, whom I will name Innocent.

Mr. Woodcock Carp and Alexis get acquainted somewhere, and she told him she would love to move in with him. Mr. Woodcock Carp said, "Sounds like a plan," and Alexis and her Innocent suitcase moved in permanently. Within a year and a half, Alexis and Regular Jail Carp took Mr. Woodcock Carp for all he was worth. They maxed out his credit cards, spent his cash, sold his furniture, auctioned his stereo equipment, and gave what was not worth selling to Mr. Goodwill and Mr. Goodwrench. Mr. Woodcock Carp was left penniless. He didn't even get visiting privileges with Innocent suitcase, which was what he really wanted. Regular Jail Carp, Alexis, and Innocent suitcase were out of Mr. Woodcock Carp's life forever. No charges could be pressed or ironed out since Mr. Woodcock Carp lost his will with his spine.

What a sad story. I thought this kind of soap opera only happened on daytime dramas. My heart really ached when he confessed the loss of his money was nothing compared to losing Innocent suitcase. He had never been married before and had no children, so she meant the most to him. Mr. Woodcock Carp actually had a heart with more than one chamber. So with this thought in mind, I decided to extend Mr. Woodcock Carp's time and gave him a "Get-Out-of-Jail-Free" card. We exchanged phone numbers and e-mail addresses and agreed to see each other soon.

Soon happened soon, as within the next week. It is July, the weather is hot, and the cell phone call details included push mowing and cutting the grass. Mr. Woodcock Carp told me it was so hot he had to sit down a few times for feeling faint. I mentioned earlier he was a thin, athletic-looking Fish, but now I am reevaluating his stature. He was really a skinny kind of old man. His age was not the factor, since he was only a couple of years younger than me, but it was his extremely skinny build. Cutting the grass had overextended his limits with regard to stretching, pushing, walking, and heavy breathing. He then told me he had to go into the house due to severe cramping and a bout of diarrhea. I had never discussed diarrhea with a single man (or any men outside of my immediate family). It seemed Mr. Woodcock Carp does not understand "too much information."

Soon happened soon again, with another phone call. This conversation was a repeat of the first conversation. It seemed Mr. Woodcock Carp was obsessed with mowing his lawn, sweating, fainting, heavy breathing, and bouts of diarrhea. He then asked if he could call me back a third time because he had to use the "pooper" again. Visions of the poo poo platter express and the train kept him moving in the direction of the bathroom.

We finally had a conversation where we actually made a fishing date. This was a new slate for a fishing escape. We agreed to meet at a karaoke bar and grill at eight o'clock the following Saturday.

Saturday arrived and so did we. First on the agenda for entertainment were two couples who were completely drunk, as in "hammered." I love to use the word "hammered" when I can. It has such a funny ring (or maybe it is a pounding sound). Anyway, they were drinking out of the biggest bongs I had ever seen. I had no idea how many they had had prior to our arrival, but the waitress kept filling them. Maybe she was related to the two gals, who I will refer to as the Bong Sisters.

Next, the Bong Sisters decided to sing Pat Benatar's "Hit Me with Your Best Shot." They laughed a lot, sang not much at all, and staggered all over the place. It was really quite comical. Once the song was finished, they wandered over to their booth to resume drinking with their dates, the Bong Brothers. The Bong Brothers got up from the booth to let the Bong Sisters slide in when all hell broke loose. The Bong Sisters missed the booth step and fell on the floor, flat on their backs and convulsing with laughter. With legs straight up in the air, they looked ready for a pelvic. Too bad the karaoke wasn't replaying Pat Benatar's "Hit Me with Your Best Shot," since their best shot was their exposed pelvic areas. On a better day, this may have been embarrassing, but being hammered always provides a different line of protocol with regard to indecent behavior.

This could have been a horrible accident, but instead ended up being a Two Stooges short film that could have won an award at the Cannes Film Festival. Still not seated in the booth, the Bong Sisters tried a few more times. I was just about peeing my pants and checked my purse for a Depends; only a Kleenex was exposed, so that would have to do. Finally, the waitress came with the owner of the bar to escort all the Bongs out the door and off the premises. Well, there goes the entertainment.

Thus to say, the evening was delightful. The food was great, the wine—as always—was fabulous, and the entertainment was bar none. Concluding: none of tonight's entertainment would be in that bar again, bar none. This was an injustice to those who just wanted to "bong it up" for an evening. In addition, I was sure bar and grill patrons do not pay a cover charge for performing pelvics, knowing that this service is free with choice.

A few days later, I called Mr. Woodcock Carp to find out if he was still on the crapper. He was not but what came out his mouth belonged in the crapper. He told me straight up he was not interested in dating one gal and wanted to enjoy being single again. What a Carp. He was so intent in going out with me, taking off my glasses, and changing my mind with regard to the number of chambers in his heart, and then he did the expected and decided to be a Carp. I felt like telling him to take a hike to the frozen section of the nearest grocery store and buy a bag of frozen corn (no peas and carrots for this bottom feeder). I said nothing and hung up the phone.

I have to admit, I was totally peed-off and am sure his decision did not have to do specifically with me. I would never honor the credit with regard to a Carp decision. Mr. Woodcock Carp made his own stink and it will follow him as he makes his way through his list of single gals, much like a fart that did not escape from the seat of his pants. In addition, how many gals are going to listen to poop stories, which are certainly full of crap? So crap and this Carp are crossed from my list with regard to future fishing. For a short time, I think I will continue to e-mail Lover Boy. He always says the right things, is a distant lover, and does not give me crap. Carpe diem.

Epilogue: A few years ago, I bumped into Mr. Woodcock Carp, since we tend to frequent the same Polish festivals. I know he is not Polish and have no idea why he masquerades as one, but my thought is he is starving for kielbasa, pirogues, and Blatz beer. This diet has serious side effects for non-Poles. I would have told him, but he did not give an indication he was interested in colon education.

If there is a 50-50 chance that something can go
wrong, then nine times out of ten it will.

—*Paul Harvey*

The Head Shot

New mail, new male; how fun
Interesting head shot
And looks quite fun
Tells me I like your bio and your pic
Pretty dress does the trick
From the nice-looking head shot
Please write to me again, quick.

New mail, new male; how fun
Interesting questions and chatter
More nice words to add to the flatter
From the nice-looking head shot
With a smile on his face
Please write to me again, quick.

New mail, new male; how fun
With a big eye-popping question no less,
"What do you look like without your glasses?"
He asks.
From the head shot without a body
I ask,
"What do you look like from the neck down?
Does your head shot match your body shot?
Does the big head shot match a bigger body shot?"

New mail, old male; all done
I do not even care if there aren't any pants from the waist down
From the head shot with no body shot, all done.
Blocked.

A Carpet Cleaner Is Not a Sex Toy

Incoming Carp E-mail: Looking for a gal who is able to take charge not only in her life but also in mine. I smoke cigarettes, love watching Captain Kangaroo on Saturday mornings, am simple with low maintenance, and enjoy working with small appliances.

> *Women rule the world. It's not really worth fighting because they know what they're doing. Ask Napoleon. Ask Adam. Ask Richard Burton or Richie Sambora. Many a man has crumbled.*
>
> —*Jon Bon Jovi, Musician*

Introduction: Moving on to Carp number three in my dating career, and I do consider it a career since it has involved research. I was still very naïve with regard to understanding men. Initially, I entered the rivers and ponds thinking all of them were going to be fabulous, since my intent was pure. My goal was to find a companion, lover, friend, or someone to make me smile and be happy. (I forgot, by the way, that I was truly happy all by myself.) So it was at this time that Nick swam into my pond. Nick was not his name, but I thought he came in the "nick of time" and was going to save me from a life of singlehood. I met Nick while picking corn with the Ya Yas on my first-time visit to the land of nothing and after the summer of the Singles Dance. I do not blame the Ya Yas for any of this. I am a big gal and can make big mistakes all by my little self.

The Novella: Nick and I decided to do a second-time-around and meet for a weekend at his condo. He did not pay for the airfare, because the deal was I would fly out to meet him and not have to pay for a place to stay. I am a slow learner with regard to understanding men who are not a part of my immediate family, and I learned that this was a major mistake. If it sounds too good to be true, then it is too good to be true. Also, I made a second mistake and that is to never accept money (or the equivalency of money, like a free condo stay). The stay may be a stay of execution. There will always be a catch, and it usually attaches itself to an unsuspecting gal.

So I went up in the air, came back onto the ground, and arrived to meet Nick in the land of nothing. Meeting was smiles, thoughts of great expectations, and a nice drive to his condo. As far as the condo, I was thinking nice, neat, cool bachelor pad. Well, none of this was the case (with the exception of the bachelor pad, or it may have been closer to a lily pad). My observation was that it was an apartment unit with shared hallway facilities for laundry. It became nice, neat, and somewhat cool after my visit. If I had known any of this was about to happen, I would have never paid for the airfare. But then again, I wouldn't be able to write this chapter and learn this lesson in life about some Carp.

As soon as we arrived at the lily pad, Nick told me he was in the midst of planning a welcoming party for his new condo and needed to spend the weekend getting it ready for his relatives and friends. By getting ready, he meant shampooing all the carpeting, which included the entire condo with the exception of the bathroom. My jaw just dropped. I came to the land of corn with the intention of fishing around with Nick, not to play house. Dorothy may have been able to click her red heels and go home to Kansas, but this little gal with nonrefundable airfare was not able to cast and click a large enough fly rod to hook Kid Rock's Land of Michigan Summers. It is what it is.

Before the lights went out, while we enjoyed a little TV, Nick told me he was an early riser and wanted to get started shampooing the carpets first thing in the morning. He also enjoyed McDonald's for breakfast and loved to have a morning cigarette. In fact, he was a smoke-aholic. I do not smoke, so he said he would keep this habit in the parking lot in front of the condo. He also told me I had my own bedroom, because he needed to get some sleep. His day would not begin right if he did not have his own bed. Honestly, this is a true story.

Right now, my jaw was once again dropping. I honestly had expected to come to the land of corn to be courted. I was so naïve, and of course, I had not met this species of Carp before, since my past with single men did not have any depth or breadth. Oh, and for you *Sex in the City* fans, he also wore an eye mask when he slept, just like Carrie Bradshaw. I wonder if Big wears an eye mask. I know he does not have a separate bedroom for Carrie. They even share the floor from time to time.

The next morning, just like clockwork, Nick went to McDonald's for coffee and a breakfast sandwich and was nice enough to bring me the same. Nick had absolutely no food in his house. He did have packets of condiments and some plastic silverware. I suppose if I had to resort to eating packaged mustard and ketchup, I could use a plastic spoon to scoop it out.

With a healthy breakfast in our stomachs, Nick then told me he had no idea of what to do in order to shampoo the carpeting. I was in shock. I thought he at least had this figured out, but he had no game plan. I told him he could rent a carpet shampooer and buy soap at a local grocery store. He looked stupefied. Like really! I thought I was having a conversation with Paris Hilton and her "teeny weenie doggie in her itty bitty tee," but I am sure she does not shampoo her carpets. Pink, one of my favorite rocker gals, has lyrics in one of her songs referring to her as "stupid girl," so I am sure there are stupid Carp.

For the next event of the day, we went off to rent a vacuum and buy soap. Upon our return, I told Nick the furniture had to go somewhere. Again, he looked at me completely stupefied. This expression on Nick's face was consistent and not a good look. Since it was a nice weather day, I wanted to tell him to move all the furniture out into the parking lot. The condo neighbors could get good use out of it during their cigarette butt breaks. But I told him we could move a lot of it into the walk-in closet, and the rest of it we could figure out as we move it. I even offered my bed in my separate room, which also came with a bare dresser. The bare dresser had my mental note written, "This piece of furniture is to be used to stack furniture."

There are varying degrees of slowness, and Nick operated on the negative spectrum of the slowest gear. There seemed to be a lot of space in his brain, so to organize his thoughts was not a part of any process.

I took one look at him and saw that if anything was going to get done, it was going to be up to me. Besides, I didn't fly all the way to nowhere to do tasks for someone else. I at least wanted to enjoy part of my stay, and part of this was with Nick, I thought.

I began by packing lamps and tables into the walk-in-closet and threw small rugs on the dresser in my room. I also stacked my bed with all of Nick's little things that added up to one big thing, so I don't have to use it. Nick had a king-size bed, and there was absolutely no reason for me to sleep in that little room by myself. Once again, I had to remind myself he liked to sleep alone and wear an eye mask and ear plugs. There would be no sleeping in his bed that night. Actually, the thrill was kind of gone, and we weren't even listening to B. B. King.

Now the cleaning began. I hated to completely take charge and emasculate Nick, so I waited to see if he was going to begin the shampooing process or if he was looking to me. Of course, he looked to me. I showed him how to fill the water and how to measure the soap. I began the shampooing and in the process went through one cup of the soap. Since the carpet was filthy, this only took a minute. I told him he could shampoo the rest by himself since I had planned to watch a Saturday afternoon football game. I sat watching the game while Nick, dressed only in his tidy whites and a long bathrobe with no belt, methodically and slowly walked back and forth shampooing the carpeting.

By the time the game was over, Nick was finished shampooing. We had nowhere to sit, or really move, since the entire carpeting was wet, except for under the sofa. So that was where we planted ourselves. We had not sat for very long when Nick got up and went into the bedroom. Still wearing only his underwear and bathrobe, he returned with the largest and longest vibrator I had ever seen. If fact, the only vibrators I had ever seen were on "Sex in the City," and those resembled giant penises. Nick's vibrator looked like an extension of the carpet cleaner. I looked at him and wondered what he planned to clean next. He had no trouble figuring out his next project, which ended up being me. The remainder of the afternoon was spent cleaning nooks and crannies that were not a part of any of the condo surfaces.

The evening ended with pizza, some flick I can't remember, and wine (which I do remember). Once again, he brought out the appliance and was interested in more nooks and crannies. With this going on, I was also thinking of the condo neighbors. Nick's unit, and I am referring to the lily pad, did not have thick walls. If I can hear people talking on the outside, I am sure they can hear my pleasure coming from the inside. I wonder how many "Oh my, oh my, oh my" qualify as a complete sentence. I will never be sure, since the batteries died.

The last event before lights out was trying to figure how a six-foot, seven-inch large economy-size man could comingle with a five-foot, three-inch no-economy gal. We actually stared at each other in a state of undress and could not figure out a road map to the nearest highway entrance. I told him his jalopy was too big and my carport was not available. Nick wrote a reminder on a sticky note to pick up batteries with breakfast. We both congratulated the night with lights out and with the mastery of an appliance that is truly a "must have" and should come equipped in all households along with hedge trimmers, weed whackers, and dust busters.

Morning came and the routine of coffee, breakfast sandwich, and a cigarette began again. He told me he planned to spend a little time in the parking lot, smoking with his condo friends. Why did I not put the furniture in the parking lot? At least if I had done this, the neighbors could have helped put the furniture back in place. Instead, I wiggled as fast as a blue gill trying to outswim a giant Tiger Musky and moved all the furniture by myself.

Quiet Riot and "bang your head, wake the dead" could not ignite enough enthusiasm to register a negative 1 on the Richter scale. Nick barely acknowledged my effort. We sat on the couch and then something popped out of my mouth that should be considered blasphemy. I asked him if we could see each other again. Nick's reply was that he was getting back with Ursula. Did you hear that? Nick was getting back with Ursula! She was breaking up with her lover of hammers and saws, namely, Construction Carp, and wanted Nick back. My only thought was that she was missing his appliance and needed to get her batteries recharged.

Nick was very lucky I am a sane and safe person. Another gal might have housed his balls in a Ziploc bag made for fish eggs. I began to totally understand the premise of "Married with Children." I was sitting next to Al, and I was Peg, and we were not even married with children.

Blasphemy. I was Peg … more blasphemy. The neighbors smoking cigarettes in the parking lot were Bud and Kelly … more blasphemy. Was there a dog in the house to complete this scene?

From this carpet cleaning episode, one could safely assume I seemed desperate or just Sarah Plain and Tall stupid. Sarah, Plain and Tall is a children's book written by Patricia MacLachlan, and the winner of the 1986 Newbery Medal. The book explores themes of loneliness and abandonment and my complementary emotional fit during times of loss. Sarah was my heart felt friend and magically arrived when she knew I needed her the most. The stupid is all about me, since I am once again in a situation in which I have no control. The fact of the matter is, I truly did not know any better, and I really wanted to spend some time with a fella who did not sort frozen vegetables or was fixated with the crapper. Blind ambition is better than no ambition.

My Ya Yas said Nick was a nice guy and, from their perspective, he was (and still is). Just because someone is nice doesn't exclude them as a possible Carp. Maybe Nick is just a matter-of-fact Carp, and "censorship" is a word that was not a part of his vocabulary. Maybe gals only last as long as the batteries. Once the batteries have died, so does he. He must go back to Mr. Battery for more positive and negative connections before his package is once again recharged. His shelf-life comes without a warranty and certainly without an extension.

In the end, I have to sincerely admit I do smile when I think of this experience. Go Ursula! Maybe the both of you are smoking cigarettes and watching Captain Kan Kan Kangaroo. Now don't tell me, you've nothing to do.

Epilogue: I continued to e-mail and phone Nick, since it was difficult to get him and his instrument of love out of my head. During our correspondences, I never once heard him mention Ursula, but I could hear the theme music to Captain Kangaroo in the background. Maybe he was talking to me while she was having a cigarette in the parking lot with the condo neighbors. Now don't tell me they've nothing to do.

Do you know these people? They got into the gene [fishing] pool while the lifeguard wasn't watching.

—*Author Unknown*

Money Trumps Compassion

Incoming Carp E-mail: Attractive, middle-aged man, excellent physical shape, a good listener, positive behaviors, and known for my great sense of humor. I am interested in a professional gal who is willing to devote time to a relationship and is also assertive when making phone calls to indicate availability.

> *But then one is always excited by descriptions of money changing hands. It's much more fundamental than sex.*
>
> —*Nigel Dennis*

Introduction: After three strikes and I'm out, I made the decision to enlist the assistance of a paid dating service. This was difficult, to say the least, since I was putting decisions (and money) in someone else's hands. Feeling like a failure at dating and thinking from the outset it was going to be much easier with no challenges, I thought this was the best way to eliminate Carp and to catch the so-called "Big One."

The Novella: My first and only date with Belly Ache Carp was a recommendation from the Money Trumps Compassion Corporation, otherwise known as any paid dating service that serves no better fare than online Carp. From the outset of signing my contract with Money Trumps Compassion, I can safely say I was blind and dumb, and I had a little cash. I should have spent the money on a sauna. I think they both cost about the same amount.

Belly Ache and I met at my favorite bar and grill. He was the first Carp I dined with at this particular establishment, so the stink factor of mackerel fumes was not present; it takes a few Carp to stink up a place. Bringing Carp to the same establishment for consecutive fishing of more than two dates within the same month is above the quota. Therefore, no more than one date a month can be attempted at any one particular bar and grill.

Belly Ache was already seated when I arrived. He had given the waitress my name so she immediately knew where I was to be seated. He made a good first impression: thin, somewhat attractive, and nicely dressed in a business suit. This being said does not necessarily guarantee Fish will be served with dinner.

The first words out of Belly Ache's mouth dissolved any appearance I would even remotely consider attractive. The fishing, or rather Carping, began with Belly Ache expressing extreme displeasure about Money Trumps Compassion. He rambled on about their unjust manner of making decisions and choices with pairing Fish or Carp. They work from the top to the bottom instead of the bottom up and believe in no desirable outcomes for bottom feeders.

This disclosure was completely uncomfortable, since I was new to the game of paid fishing with Carp sponsored by Money Trumps Compassion. I decided he was going to pay for the meal, since he made me feel like a prostitute. Rendering my services of being a good listener, courtesy, and manners could be considered prostitution. Payment was in the form of dinner, drinks, and immobilizing my spirit into submission.

Belly Ache continued by complaining that the Big Boss of Money Trumps Compassion had a few strict "Thou Shalt Nots," of which the number one, according to ranking or "fish scales," states, "Thou Shalt Never Surprise Me with an Unexpected Personal Visit." The second fish scale is "Thou Shalt Only Contact Me by Phone": If your phone call is not returned, then understand you have been deemed bottom feeder status, known as Carp. These were two "Thou Shalt Nots" Belly Ache broke early in his fishing career, and he was now considered a stinking carcass with no special privileges.

The misery began when Belly Ache was matched with a Caffler, which is a collector of bones and rags; he liked her a lot, but the feeling was not mutual. He mentioned that he wiggled his big tail and flapped his big lips and was interested in many more fishing events. Girly Caffler

29

worked many hours collecting bones and rags and said she did not have time to spend with a demanding Carp. Additionally, she told him his smell was worse than any bones or rags she had ever collected.

Of course, Belly Ache's feelings were hurt, and he did a double-check of his armpits to see if they really did stink worse than bones and rags. He even discreetly smelled his private parts, which were also fine. What he did not know was the smell came from within. All he needed to do was exhale and the exhaust from his privates would expel. This theory of respiration is true for all bottom feeders. In the end, Girly Caffler slipped through Belly Ache's net, and he made the mistake of losing his first prime fillet.

Belly Ache's second fishing experience involved a lovely seventy-year-old Capillaire Maker (this occupation deals with making syrup flavored with orange and is used in making health drinks). Capillaire Maker stated right up front that she does not telephone Fish. Belly Ache said this is fine, but he would prefer a call from her to understand if she was really interested in him as a catch. She asserted a firm no and said he had better forget about her. Both she and Lady Gaga had their "head and heart on the dance floor" and were "sick and tired of" their phones ringing. This date would be the only one she would be able to fit into her calendar for the next two years. Syrup collecting and dancing with the Gaga is much more lucrative than deboning Carp. In the end, Capillaire Maker also slipped through Belly Ache's net, another loss of a prime fillet.

After losing two prime fillets, Belly Ache decided to pay a visit to the Money Trumps Compassion Corporation. He completely forgot about the "Thou Shalt Nots" and the fish scales in descending order that become the demise of bottom feeders. He added insult to injury by showing up with mackerel balls, sheep head lips, and chum.

The receptionist greeted Belly Ache with her Passionate Voice, not to be confused with compassion, telling him Big Boss Money Trump was not available, will never be available, and he should have known this when he signed the one million word contract. Belly Ache opened his big mouth and stretched his even bigger rubbery lips and smiled, saying he just wanted a moment of time to straighten a few things out with regard to the lineage of Fish and their choice in pairing. Passionate Voice said, "No, under no circumstances will we bend the rules on your behalf. We are famous for picking your gals from the most desirable pool, and if they are not attracted to your scales, it is no fault of ours."

Belly Ache fell off the deep end of the sandbar and went into a tirade, saying, "I liked the Caffler and the Capillaire Maker, but they could not fit me into their schedules. Why are you signing up gals with no calendar time? Why aren't you finding me gals who love a Belly Acher? Why aren't there gals who call me and consider it a 'turn-on'? And what is this about the 'stink factor'? I can't smell anything anywhere near my perimeter. For Pete's sake, both gals were seventy years old, hot, and professionals. They are what I am looking for. I never thought seventy-year-old gals were hot prior to these fishing events. Can't you demand they give me a second chance? I'll even bring them mackerel balls, sheep head lips, and chum."

I was repulsed. I had not had any experience with this species of Carp and truly didn't know what to do. I kept thinking that the longer I hung in and listened, things would turn around and Belly Ache would figure out I was the new gal on the dock of the bay with Otis Redding singing back-up. Belly Ache had no interest in me. I was just a bobber on the end of a pole waiting for the next hit.

Passionate Voice continued, saying she could not rebook previous gals. With regard to all this pomp and circumstance, she would send his information to Big Boss Money Trump for consideration and a possible review. In the meantime, new gals will be served with his next fishing. The sad news was the new gal ended up being me. It was hard to fathom that Big Boss Money Trump would do something so mean to a new gal. I hadn't even been egged and breaded, and I was already designated as the "shut up this Carp" or else no trout for you.

I can actually hear Big Boss Money Trump saying, "This is a test and only a test. For the next sixty seconds, the dating service is conducting a test to see if you understand we can only serve what we have acquired. If we only have Carp, then we can only serve Carp. Everything is out of our control, with the exception of your fee. I am advising you only once to buy a sauna instead."

At the end of dinner, and yes there was dinner, since I am a prostitute and demand payment for services rendered, Belly Ache asked me what I was going to do about the Money Trumps Compassion Corporation. I told him he was my first Fish and I did not think his breaking of any

"Thou Shalt Nots" applied to me. I was confident that Belly Ache was a big mistake and compassion would trump money. There had to be more than a fee when choosing a paid dating service. Maybe my second Fish would be different since I had already passed on the sauna.

Belly Ache gave me a follow-up phone call to see if I had raised hell with the Money Trumpers. I told him no, and finally to put him out of the pond, I told him if he ever had to go to a wedding or an event, then I would be the gal for him. I love dress-up and can socialize. One rule of caution I told him was I always drove my own car since I made the decision in determining when to leave. From this fishing, I learned it is fine to just get up and leave. There is no need for excuses, and a polite smile will do.

Epilogue: Belly Ache continued to ache his complaints throughout the summer. I wished I had had more of a will with my spine during this time but the fact of the matter is, I did not. Understanding being single is an evolution. In the early stages, I did not understand how to put myself out there; it is an experiment, just like giving birth the first time. Some things work, and then there are other times when it is necessary to visit the drawing board with *Harold and His Purple Crayon* and draw a question mark, asking Miss Barbara and her magic mirror from Romper Room, circa 1955, for advice. For you younger folks, you could probably get pretty good advice just by watching "The View."

> *There is as much difference between a mackerel and a*
> *red mullet as there is between a miller and a bishop.*
>
> —*Baron Leon Brisse (1813–1876)*

The Lazy Days of Dukes
with Carp Dukey

Incoming Carp E-mail: I am a man of small means and enjoy the simple life and love of nature. Also, as a simple man, I prefer snail mail versus technology, conservative clothing, and quiet nights at home in front of the fireplace.

> *When a man of forty falls in love with a girl of twenty,*
> *it isn't her youth he is seeking but his own.*
>
> —*Lenore Coffee*

Introduction or B.C. (before Cindy) Carp Dukey's life to date: Carp Dukey, alias Mr. Married Carp, alias Carpe Diem, was difficult to fish with since he had a cell phone in a dead-zone area and lived in the middle of a pond without an easy access. Prior to our initial fishing, Carp Dukey was (and still is) married to Lazy Dukes, not her real name but the moniker suits her image. Carp Dukey was married prior to Lazy Dukes but left his wife of thirty years because he became smitten with a woman who was twenty years younger than him. Lazy swept Dukey off his feet with her lazy attitude towards life; her short, short cut-off jeans; and her "Daisy Dukes bikini on top." She seemed like a dream from heaven, since Lazy did not require any maintenance. For all practical purposes, Carp Dukey and Lazy Dukes had a relationship from Hazzard and were living the life of Inglorious Bastards. Their life is not to be confused with Quentin Tarantino and his *Inglorious Basterds*.

The Novella: After Belly Ache, I decided to try another Fish from another paid dating service. I didn't see any sense in putting all my Carp in one pail. U2 sings my fishing theme song: "I still haven't found what I'm looking for."

Carp Dukey was the catch of the day, and we decided to meet at the Rustic Floor Saloon for their famous Peanut-crusted Sheep Head. I could always skip the peanut crust and throw it on the floor like any other local saloon if I wanted to get right down to the Carp. I wondered why the establishment didn't post a sign telling customers to do so in the first place.

Meeting Carp Dukey began well. He arrived in his pickup and did look nice in his cuffed jeans, polo shirt, and the beginning of a grizzly beard. He was shorter than I liked, since I struggle with guys who may suffer from the Napoleon Syndrome. I haven't met any short men I actually liked, but then again, I haven't met many men. Also, he did not say much, smiled a lot, and seemed shy and reserved. This was refreshing since I was on overload with a headache from Belly Ache.

We began by establishing boundaries with regard to payment of the tab and decided to pay separately. Since I was paying, I ordered a glass of wine to accompany the sheep head. Carp Dukey ordered a draft beer with his exact order of the bottom feeder. The evening went quickly with a couple of drinks, talk, laughter, and a meal I will never order again. There is nothing special you can do to prepare a bottom feeder as an entree. No breading, flaking, deep frying, or steaming can disguise a piece of Carp. We both agreed on the bad menu choice and decided to fish again the next Saturday at five o'clock at a different establishment, the counterpart saloon known as the Rustic Ceiling. Carp Dukey told me his friend, Amboy Dukes, swore by the menu as favorable. With a name like that, I am not sure I trust his judgment (the Amboy Dukes were Detroit acid rockers from the late 1960s).

Saturday arrived and the second fishing began with Carp Dukey and me looking at the menu. I was starving since, as a religious runner, I had run nine miles in the morning and waited all day for a menu honored by the great Amboy Dukes. Dukey seemed like a squirming minnow in shallow water. I was a little miffed by this attitude, since we had already met once. Quickly, I assessed my attire, since I knew from the dating service that Carp Dukey was not fond of exposed breasts, of which I had none, and raggedy cut-off jeans. I was wearing a camisole and a skort so I was good in both departments.

Carp Dukey broke the silence by informing me that he already had dinner with his father, who he visited regularly, and he would only order a Coke. Something did not seem right. Why would he agree to a dinner date if he was not going to eat? Pushing this aside, I decided to order the fish and chips and a glass of wine. The fish menu said halibut, so I thought I was safe from indigestion or picking large bones from my teeth and the back of my throat.

Halfway through a fork full of halibut, Dukey told me he was still married. I tried hard not to choke. With no Plan B in my bra, Swiss Army knife, or pepper spray, I waited to hear the rest of the story.

I digressed and thought maybe at the beginning of fishing we should hand each other an inventory and check what will be on the agenda for fishing. Examples include storytelling, fabricating, hallucinating, laughing, drinking, shocking, dulling the senses, and who pays the tab are good for starters from my experience, since Peas and Carrots was quite shocking and Nick was pretty much dull. Both parties get to list two in order and see if they agree. If there is no agreement, then "Go Fish" is allowed one more time. If there is no agreement on the second time, there is no third base and home plate, and fishing is done. This is a much easier way to put two people out of their misery or a better way to define what shall be included with fishing.

Carp Dukey decided storytelling was on the invisible inventory and began with his meeting of Lazy Dukes at the Rustic Ceiling in the company of Amboy Dukes. Even though he was still married to the first Mrs. Carp Dukey, he told me he could not take his eyes off of Lazy, who was twenty years younger and had a valley of cleavage deeper than the Mid-Atlantic Ridge. He couldn't think of anything other than burying his head in that deep ridge and not coming up for air. From this information, I am pretty sure "not coming up for air" means he is not going to have an orgasm. What is the point of burying a head in big boobs and not being able to climax? It seems like a wasted effort. Thank goodness I am small breasted. Anyway, Carp Dukey goes home to Mrs. Carp Dukey and tells her he wants a divorce and she can have

35

everything of his, which is nothing. I wonder if her boobs are more than nothing.

After a year and a half of marriage to Lazy, things are more than dried up like smoked chub hanging on a stringer. Life with Lazy is nothing like life with June Cleaver. For you younger gals, just think of someone who is wholesome, does everything right, and wears a dress when cooking, maybe like Kelly Ripa. Lazy does not cook, clean, or make her man feel satisfied. Their entire life is spent traveling the circuit of bar and grills so she can show off her stuff to other Carp. She loves to do this in the presence of Carp Dukey. Humiliation and degradation are the trump cards of her game in making him feel smaller than a grain of sand swallowed by a clam.

Carp Dukey says they are now separated but cannot dive into the Big D, which is the Big Divorce, since he has no money, because no money went to the first Mrs. Carp Dukey, for which there was also none. How in the heck does this happen to me? I guess when throwing myself out to the Fish with only flapping rubbery-lipped Carp available, too much information becomes the big agenda item. Actually, too much information can be a good thing. Knowing big breasts are an enticing way for a Carp to smother himself to death certainly has helped me decide never to get a boob job. How would I explain to my grown sons a man died in my valley of no return and I am eating Froot Loops in the county jail?

My head and heart are divided into three gray areas. The first is betrayal, the second is the scapegoat, and the third is blame. Betrayal is definitely in the picture. I feel betrayed because he did agree to a second date. He chose to divulge personal information to a single gal who has no intention of mixing up Carp by including the married species. This information should have been shared with the money handlers, of which Carp Dukey has none. He must have used Amboy's credit card since he has no credit, no spine, and no will. The money handlers definitely did not do their math homework, and he should have never been allowed into the fishing pond. I also feel I am the scapegoat, since he successfully escaped his ruined life and shortcomings with the use of his time on my clock. Lastly, I feel blame because maybe my attire triggered this scene. Yes, I was wearing a camisole and a short skort, and maybe in his pea head of a brain and one-chamber heart he put me into the same fishing bowl as Lazy. It is possible all of the above are not true, but it is possible that all of the above are true. I cannot figure out Carp and am telling myself all this has nothing to do specifically with me.

I tell Carp Dukey I will pay for his Coke and I have to leave. I know he doesn't have any money, and the quicker this Carp event is over, the better. It cost me thirty-five dollars, and the only thing I enjoyed was the wine. I promise the next thirty-five dollars I spend will be for online shopping at J.C. Penny, Macy's, or Victoria's Secret. In doing so, I always walk away from my computer with a smile on my face and with money well spent.

Epilogue: Once again, I find myself wondering if finding a partner or a companion is really important. I am no closer to the "Big One" than when I started. Maybe there is no "Big One." Maybe the "Big One" is Nemo, or better yet, Bruce the Shark from *Jaws*.

Sometimes I wonder if men and women really suit each other. Perhaps they should live next door and just visit now and then.

—*Katharine Hepburn*

My Life's in Jeopardy, Baby

Incoming Carp E-mail: I am interested in a well-maintained gal who desires a much older Fish with a slight athletic build. My favorites include cycling, red meat, carbohydrates, Zinfandel wine, and good night kisses.

> *Graze on my lips; and if those hills be dry, stray*
> *lower, where the pleasant fountains lie.*
>
> —*William Shakespeare*

Introduction: The *Price Is Right, Truth or Consequences,* and *Wheel of Fortune* are all games of chance. They are games of guessing and sometimes pure luck. This story happened to take place when I was once bitten, twice shy from a few *Uno mas no mas* paid-for dates. I am now at number three of exchanging cash with the money handlers and hoping for a *Wheel of Fortune* and may be fortunate enough to land a "Big One" hook, line, and sinker. Chance was his name; a cool name may bring a cool guy and not a Carp. So it is with Carping Chance, I will dance my way through this fishing quagmire. Hopefully, our encounter will not resemble Jeopardy.

The Novella: Carping Chance was a match from another reliable dating service. This fishing site was not a place of escorts or Johns, but a legitimate service for gals who think by paying a fee they might catch a rainbow trout or walleye. This is not so. Whether it is a free dating service or a paid service, a Carping Chance can come from anywhere.

Money does not determine the possible number of chances a gal may encounter.

To begin with, I was very hesitant when considering Carping Chance, since he was nine years older than me. As a long-distance runner, I was wondering if by chance he could catch me. But as an older Fish to begin with, is nine years' difference really a big difference? What does nine years look like? What does a nine-year-old child look like to a newborn? What does a nineteen-year-old youth look like to a ten-year-old? What does a thirty-one-year-old look like to a twenty-two-year-old? Since the nine years older and the nine years younger may not care, is there really any difference? On the flip side of the coin, if any of these three scenarios were considering fishing, the age difference may be considered *The Perfect Storm*

I tried to work through the aging anxiety by asking myself the sixty-four-million-dollar million questions. What do his teeth look like? Are they yellow, crooked, large, or dentures? How big are his ears? A former student once told me the ears are the only part of the body that continually grows until the day we die. I was truly amazed by his comment and accepted the statement at face value. This truly explains why I have seen many older men with huge ears resembling megaphones, cauliflower, cabbage, and best yet, *The Little Shop of Horrors*. In each instance, it is easy to imagine being swallowed whole and never to be seen again. I never once looked at the research, but my student's comment seemed plausible and so is my question with regard to big ears.

Additionally, how does he dress and what about his eyes? Is his normal attire khakis pulled above his waist, as if he is running from flood waters or a suit? Are his eyes yellow? I don't know why the whites of the eyes of older men turn yellow, almost jaundice-like. What is even worse is when the red blood vessels appear. Their eyes seem to be a road map of their past life, or maybe it is really many lives. Maybe both cats and Carp come with a total of nine since they both have the natural instinct of eating prey.

Finally, what about his butt? Butts are stranger on older men. Most of them do not even have a butt, or it sags or just hangs as a flap of loose skin. I wonder if this is where the phrase "flapping in the breeze" came from. Looking at some men from the side view, their butts are almost nonexistent. How does this happen? Is it from the many years of squatting and trying to see under women's dresses as they are standing next to a café table or coming down the fire escape of a burning building? My childhood friend Danny was the first one down the fire escape during a fire drill and saw my underwear up close and personal. He ended up in the principal's office for the afternoon. Maybe if more boys were caught by the principal when they were exhibiting this behavior they could have saved their asses and not resemble a dollar fish from the side view.

Even though all these thoughts were in my head, none of these questions reached my lips. Yes, I am superficial from the outset and a believer in first impressions. Aren't we all? I am sure Carp do the same mental undressing of us gals. We are all the same when it comes to undressing others with our naked eyes. Maybe we should refer to them as "private eyes." Maybe the Pink Panther will come to our rescue with a large pair of shades and a billed cap to cover our private thoughts.

Consistently, the service assured me Carping Chance was a good catch. Even as an older Fish, he cycled to keep in shape. I told them I am not into spandex and molded private parts. We true-blue runners are on the other side of the fence from hard core cyclists. I would never refer to them as "Bikers" and reserve this name to hard core Harley Hogs.

The service continued with a final lure by telling me Carping Chance was well educated and well read. In his past work, he was a valuator, or a person who sets the price on valued goods and is admired for his or her forthrightness. Also, talking with him would be easy since he had a lot of knowledge about many things. I know many Carp who know a little about a lot of things. I also know Carp who know a lot about nothing. Is Carping Chance one of those Carp who are walking Google search engines? Maybe he is a Yahoo.

The service wore me down with their fillet knife, and I succumbed to fishing with Carping Chance. He called, and our first impressions formed from the sound of our voices. His voice seemed friendly and a little gruff, like he was gargling with gravel or chewing on rhinestones, or may have smoked as a habit since he was ten. I doubt the smoking, since he is a cyclist, but you never know. Many avid golfers drink on the course while they are driving golf carts. The same may hold true for cyclists since they, too, are on a vehicle with wheels and steering.

With resolution, he definitely sounded older, but I promised myself to get past these preconceived notions and to put my best Sketcher foot forward. We agreed to meet at a local bar and grill located on a nearby lake. This was a good choice, since I have not dined there in the past with previous Carp, so the sink factor will not be present.

Since the dining is casual, I dressed in a nice, flattering pair of capris, a trendy top, and my wonderful Sketcher sandals. It was warm, so I grabbed a light sweater. I was early to the bar and grill and waited for Chance in the lobby. I watched various people walk in and even approached a man who was looking at wines in the wine shop and asked if he was Chance. He said, "No, but I can be if you want me to." This made me smile.

So I sat back down in the lobby and waited. A few minutes passed, and an older gentleman, dressed in a Ralph Lauren suit and the biggest pair of black dress shoes I have ever seen, entered and gave the hostess his name. I got up from my seat and introduced myself. He smiled. I was struggling to get past his shoes. The suit was fine, even though it was out of place, but the orthopedic shoes were challenging.

At three years of age, I had polio for seven months and was crippled. I remember very clearly seeing many of the kids in the hospital fitted with braces and big, round-toed shoes. This was trauma for me then and is still trauma for me now. Fortunately, I did not have any long-term side effects after receiving the Salk vaccine except for the recurrent dreams of needles and big-toed shoes. My thoughts were with asking him about his big shoes, but decided it would be an invasion of his privacy. Maybe he, too, has recurrent dreams of needles and big-toed shoes and wears the foot gear as his Big Badge of Honor. All these "maybes" are none of my business on a first fishing date. Hopefully, big, round-toed shoes will not define Chance as a species of Carp.

The conversation began with Carping Chance telling me about his cycling and that he was a here, there, and everywhere biking guy. He was retired and able to take off on his bike first thing in the morning and did not return until dark. I looked at him and believed all his words. This explained his skinny, scrawny build. I was sure if we were ever to get intimate I would break him apart like a toothpick. He would certainly fall and not be able to get up. I would have to spend the rest of the night reassembling his body parts, and it has been forty years since I took high school physiology. I do know that the ulna and the radius are connected to the funny bone and that the tibia and fibula are connected to the femur, so at least I would be able to get his legs and arms back together. Humpty Dumpty would have to do the rest.

All this cycling talk was not working for me so I changed the conversation to the wine list. Carping Chance enjoyed wine and decided to tell me everything he knows, and we were once again having a one-sided conversation. He began with the Zinfandel, and I mentioned it is one of my favorites. He then defined the difference between Zinfandel and white Zinfandel. White Zinfandel is really Kool-Aid fake wine, and Zinfandel is truly a red wine. Even though I did know the difference, he made me feel as if my background of wine came from the movie *Sideways* with Thomas Haden Church in charge of the wine knowledge, of which he was not. He was in charge of having a naked biker chase him down the street because he left his wallet behind after fornicating with the big biker's wife, who was also of the large economy size. If you have not seen this movie, it is a must. I am confident you will come away with a much deeper appreciation of Michelangelo's statue of David.

Finally, the waitress arrived and Carping Chance ordered a massive onion cheeseburger with a huge load of French fries. Onions are a stretch for me unless I am in the privacy of my home. This choice told me either his breath is immune to the charge of the onion odor brigade or he just doesn't care. I ordered a fish sandwich and French fries, knowing I planned to get drunk because I ordered fish in the presence of a Carp.

Our food arrived as Carping Chance announced that three of his wives left him because they could not stand him. His fourth wife joined a religious cult, and he considered this fall-out as an annulment and a marriage that did not count. He continued and told me he had been a valuator for thirty-six years and hated every moment: the arguing, the price setting, and the impact it had on his married lives dooming him to a life of cycling, making condescending remarks, divorcing wives, and drinking gallons of red Zinfandel from the well pump in his back yard. The consequences of his past have made him who he is in the present and have determined his future. I couldn't stand him either, and I only knew him for little more than half an hour. I was spending way too much time with a valuator who had no marital values.

After his omissions, he told me he liked the way things turned out and his choice of doom and gloom with consequences. He liked the financial freedom and the fact he can cycle around the globe on a regular basis. I wondered if his bike cycled on water when he came to an ocean. I was not sure if he had tried to befriend anyone with redeeming qualities that would allow him to walk on water. In conclusion, Chance was a Carp, and I was not jumping into deep waters with him again. How on earth did he even think he could pick up a gal with his litany of woe-be-gones. Either he did not take Enticing Gals 101 or he just did not know better. I could handle the not knowing better, since he was an adult male.

In the end, Carping Chance was a gentleman Carp and picked up the tab. It was dark and he walked me to my car. I was just about to open the door when he held me by my shoulders and gave me a great big, dry cardboard kiss. I thought I was going to crack like a stone tablet. Maybe this after-dinner scene was a reenactment from the "Eleventh Commandment." Moses delivered the Ten Commandments, so maybe we lesser mortals hold the other tablets. Somehow, I can see this Eleventh Commandment: "Thou shalt not drink red wine with valuators." My hope was that I would be pardoned, I would have a front row seat in heaven, and the red wine served with my last supper would not be Zinfandel.

Epilogue: Carping Chance continued to call me in the weeks that followed. As a believer in second chances, I gave Carping Chance a second more of my time. The plan was that he would cycle over to my house, and we would take my car to another bar and grill for lunch. My thoughts were with regard to cycling and the stink factor, because I know what I smell like after I run. I asked him if he would like to shower prior to our lunch date. He said no and that he always traveled with a towel to wipe off the sweat. Nice.

With Carping Chance's arrival, I met him in the garage and we exchanged hellos. I was immediately drawn to his more-than-skinny legs. I thought I had skinny legs but believe me, as in the 4 percent of people who find it difficult to lie, his legs were beyond skinny. It was like they had withered away with his butt. Maybe he got caught twice looking under girls' skirts as they were coming down the fire escape during fire drills and ended up in the principal's office to lose both his ass and his legs. I wondered how he explained this to his mother when he returned home from school that day. This certainly made it easier for me to understand why all his women divorced him. It would be difficult to have a nightly conjugal visit with no legs to straddle or ass to hang on to.

Carping Chance took out his towel from his bike sack, wiped himself down, and announced he was ready to eat cow. He was famished from the cycling, and I was hoping the food would fill some of the loose pouches on his legs. I drove, he sat beside me, and he didn't stink from sweat. This surprised me, but I guess if you have no fat you have no sweat. What in the heck was my problem then? It must be the overload of or lack of hormones from menopause.

We arrived at the bar and grill, and once again, I ordered my usual fish and a glass of wine; Carping Chance decided on a massive cow burger and an order of potato steak fries with two beers. The two beers surprised me since he would be cycling here, there, and everywhere, and at the end of the day, he had to make it home. I wondered if drinking and driving rules have the same application with cyclists. Is it possible to chase a Carping Chance in pursuit? I should send this idea to Gary Larsen for a future Far Side series using cyclists and humor. I can actually see an officer pulling Carping Chance over and telling him the carpool lane of the highway is not intended for cyclists. As a past valuator, I am sure he will argue the point, he will lose his "Get-Out-of-Jail-Free" card, and he will end up behind bars at St. James Place. My digression and back to reality.

Lunch was the same as the dinner the week before: more gravel, more dirt, more spit, and a boatload of carbohydrates marinated in opinions and biases. Carping Chance, always the gentleman with expenses, paid the tab, and we returned to my house. I was *Sarah Plain and Tall* stupid and asked him if he would like a glass of wine and to spend a few moments on the deck before he left to pedal across the other half of the planet. He said yes, and my plans for after he leaves are to research Emily Post's book with regard to etiquette and the protocol line of when enough should be enough with regard to being polite or just plain stupid; I am plain stupid.

44

I went into the house and told Carping Chance to meet me on the upper deck while I poured two glasses of white wine. It was a week day and the lake was quiet. I relished the quiet, knowing it wouldn't be long because I was sure Carping Chance's lips would soon be flapping about something negative.

We continued with the quiet moment when suddenly a jet skier appeared and gave us a show of his talents. Carping Chance went off the deep end of the sand bar with negative comments about the noise and the world's stupidest invention. My comment was that I had lived on this lake for a long time and I had pretty much gotten used to the noise and was able to block it out. In fact, I wouldn't have noticed any noise if he had not brought it to my attention. He looked at me in total amazement. It was at this point we both recognized we were from different planets, and it isn't Venus and Mars; it was AD and BC.

We finished our wine and I walked with Chance to his bike; he stood on one side with me on the other. He then leaned over and, once again, grabbed my shoulders and gave me a big cardboard kiss. Thank goodness this happened in the garage and no one else could see.

Epilogue: It was on this day I decided to remove myself from the dating scene for six months. Charlotte York from *Sex in the City* shares my heart with her words from one episode: "Where is he? I am exhausted." My life had evolved around trying to find the "Big One" with only finding Carp. Serious time needed to be spent on cleaning the house, taking out the trash, paying bills, mowing the lawn, and feeding my cats. During this time, I also took a couple South of the Border vacations and mingled with fellas who I would only see for a few days or maybe a little longer and understand, as with frozen vegetables, they go back in the freezer at the end of the week.

When I got off the soap I got offered all these, you know, "women in jeopardy"—I call them "disease of the week" movies.

—Sarah Michelle Gellar

Don't Mess with Bill

I call and I call and there is no reply
The second week comes and an answer
With reply
Out of the country for a couple of weeks
So sorry, sounds sweet.

His reply
He says his name is Bill
But this cannot be so
He says the name is his alias
And his preference instead of Will.

Meeting Bill in the lobby
Voice and face do not match
But this is true
For I have met others who
Have spoken who also do not match.

He seems jolly false
And I cannot pick up his take
Cracking so many jokes
At a rapid pace
Is it sarcasm?
Or an attitude with lack of self-confidence?

Self-confidence, no
A lawyer is Bill
He has self-esteem
To litigate and drill
A jury, a judge, and colleagues
So why this tight-lipped defense sequence?

A second meeting may tell
Why I should mess with Bill not Will
Not for me he says

He has been divorced thrice
You will not be my next to suffice
And are much too nice.

What a man
Whose honor and esteem
When meeting someone who beams
Shouldn't be looking in the medicine cabinet for pills
For the prescription will read
Don't mess with Bill.

Part II
Intermediate School: The Marathon Phase

Concentrate on small segments of your race at a time. For example, rather than obsessing about the distance that remains, simply complete the next mile in good form ... try another, then another, until the race is done.

—*Jerry Lynch*

Please Squeeze the Charmin

Incoming Carp E-mail: I enjoy golf, home repair, and dining with a companion.

Part of the reason that men seem so much less loving than women
is that men's behavior is measured with a feminine ruler.

—*Francesca M. Cancian*

Preface: A New Day: Six months later, I was refreshed and ready to begin the intermediate stage of my fishing career, the marathon stage. It was late spring, and I promised myself to assertively attack the next six months in finding the "Big One." With the time off from dating, I now felt refreshed and knew I was able to look at men more objectively. My hopes were to find him before I exceeded 26.2 Carp miles and not spend the entire summer in a bar and grill.

Introduction: For this fishing event, known as leg one or 3.7 of my 26.2-mile journey, I could include several Carp I met with whom I had similar experiences, but I chose this particular one because it took time to figure out his final status and to bestow his graduate degree from Fish to honorary Carp. Charmin, which is his Fish name, had a nice photo and interesting biography note that he was looking for a companion, so he seemed like a good species for casting the fishing rod and reel. I asked myself, why jump into looking to be wife number five when being a companion will do. I used one of my better lures and my best rod and cast my incoming interest note. Charmin took the bait and bite or maybe it is bit.

The Novella: With Charmin's bite, we exchanged phone numbers and agreed to meet at my favorite bar and grill. Arriving early, I decided to wait by the front door so he would be sure to see me. A few moments later, I spotted him walking down the street and waved. He apologized for being late since he was not exactly sure of the location. I told him he was fine with time and I had only been waiting for a few minutes. Charmin looked exactly like his photo with his head of thick black hair, solid stocky body but not in a fat way, comfortable plaid shirt and blue jeans, and I was pleased.

The waitress seated us at a booth and we ordered. I offered to pay my portion of the bill, and he told me he would take care of the tab. We ordered dinner and drinks. I do not remember what we ate or what we drank, but I do remember him. Charmin looked so comfortable, and his body looked nice and soft like a cute teddy bear or similar to huggable Charmin tissue. There was no litany of questions with answers, nothing seemed contrived, and all of our conversation felt comfortably spontaneous. At the end of dinner, he told me he did not like to dine alone and enjoyed eating with a companion. I was tempted to squeeze the Charmin but I knew it was too early in our fishing to begin the hugging stage. We agreed to meet the following week for another dinner date.

The following week arrived, and I felt comfortable enough to let Charmin pick me up at my house. I asked if he wanted to come in for a few minutes, and he said yes. Standing in the kitchen, he shared with me his interest in remodeling houses. To be more specific, he really loved to work with money pits since the end product was satisfying in that he could really see a completed work of art. Currently, he was working on the money pit of all pits. The owners, an elderly couple, were pack rats and had hoarded everything from the past seventy-plus years. Charmin said he could hardly get through the house to assess and evaluate what needed to be done in order to make the pit look like a home. He continued by telling me he had to build a maze through the trash, and trash it was since all of it belonged in the dumpster, to provide him with some semblance of a layout of the rooms and possible hazards with regard to electricity, gas, and water. He finally told the couple he could not proceed with the project until the trash was dumped. The next day, the elderly couple rented a dumpster and all the trash was gone by Charmin's next visit. His summation was that the couple may have called Mr. Goodwill and Mr. Goodwrench and told them to take everything not nailed down or related to electricity, gas, or water. To this, I added they may have put a sign reading "Everything Free" and let the locals take it all, making it even easier. Charmin laughed.

With this story, I told Charmin I was interested in remodeling my kitchen. He took a look at my countertops and gave me a few ideas of what to do with ceramic tiles and granite. Also, he knew a lot of people in the business and he could probably get me a good deal and would install it free of labor. Again, I was feeling Charmin comfortable as if we had known each other for a long time. With all of this incoming, I told him I would think about it. I had learned from others about the hazards of money, free labor, and fishing. The combination of the three can lead to a disaster when dealing with possible bottom feeders, which can become a slippery slope without a sandbar.

We left the house, and Charmin took me to a nice restaurant in town. Still feeling very comfortable, even more so, I did not make mention of the tab and decided to offer to pay after dinner. The waitress seated us at a table with a nice view of the water front. I ordered the parmesan-crusted walleye and a glass of wine, and Charmin ordered a steak and dark ale. Once again, we had a nice meal with drinks but mostly it was about not dining alone and having a companion with the experience. I offered to pay my portion of the tab, but Charmin said he had it.

The ride home was once again comfortable with spontaneous conversation. In the driveway, I was thinking about squeezing the Charmin but decided the second date was still too soon. We decided to calendar another dinner date the following Friday. As Charmin pulled out of the driveway, I felt as if I had been cast into a fishing pool filled with Charmin tissue. There is no more wonderful way to sink than in deep softness.

Next Friday arrived, and once again Charmin knocked at my door. I cannot get enough of his thick black hair, glasses, and Charmin soft looks. I love men in glasses because they are also a part of me. He also looked terrific in jeans and a sweater. I didn't know what any other gal would think, but as far as I was concerned, I was the only one who mattered.

We took the short drive to the lake bar and grill. He tells me the food and drinks are good. Even though I had been to this establishment during my elementary stage, I felt no apprehension. With a new beginning and round two of fishing, the past was the past and I could only think of this place in the present.

The waitress sat us at a table and told us she would be back shortly to take our dinner and drink order. It was late Friday night, and I was starving. I had run nine miles in the morning and had such a busy day that I did not have time to eat. Drinking without eating makes me do all the following: talk a mile a minute, slur my words, laugh uncontrollably, and become drunk quickly, to the point that a simple walk to the bathroom could become a collision course. I shared none of this with Charmin other than the mileage that I had run and the hunger pangs in my stomach.

Charmin suggested we get an appetizer of crab cakes with our drinks before we ordered dinner. He reasoned this would give us time to talk and the food would ease my hunger. Crab cakes are in my pay-it-forward memory and not a part of my pay back, since I have not yet met Mayo. You will read about this fishing adventure a little later.

The waitress brought my wine and Charmin's dark ale prior to the appetizer. Depleted from nine miles of morning running, I sucked down the wine and a glass of water like a Fish who has swallowed the hook, line, and sinker. Charmin sucked down his dark ale and ordered two more drinks, one for each of us. I asked the waitress for two more full glasses of water to accompany the wine. I felt the urge of liquid diet taking over, pushing the food aside. I knew this was due to the phenomena of drinking before eating. Too much liquid in the stomach makes no room for solids.

Our second drinks were served with the crab cake appetizer. My stomach was full of liquid, so seeing the small tablespoons of crab mixed with a heavy dose of mayo was comforting. With two glasses of wine, two glasses of water, and crab cakes, I was full up to my eyeballs.

At this point, I was seriously considering telling Charmin to forget the dinner and we should just drink the night away, but I quickly dismissed the thought. Charmin was about dinner and companionship, so he would definitely want dinner, and I planned on squeezing some

Charmin tonight. It was our third date, and for reasons only I can come up with, it was the right time of passage for squeezing.

The waitress took our dinner orders. I am a fish lover (ironic, I know), so once again, ordered the parmesan-crusted walleye, and Charmin ordered a medium-rare steak, baked potato, and side salad. He also ordered two more drinks. I sucked down two more glasses of water in preparation for the next round.

The next round was served with our dinner, thank goodness. I was full of water and wine and felt like I should be a participant in the Last Supper. My thoughts were about asking the waitress for a loaf of bread, but decided this would be inappropriate and indicate that my brain was the size of a grape.

Dinner conversation began with lessons with regard to a medium-rare steak. Charmin called the waitress over and told her the steak was bloody enough that the drippings could be misconstrued as the soup de jour. She smiled and said she would return with what he asked for in the first place, minus the soup. Second time around was the charm. Charmin now had a good meal, good drinks, comfortable conversation, and a dinner partner.

While we were eating, I had enough of a frame of mind to figure the tab total was close to one hundred dollars. Three drinks each, two appetizers, and two complete dinners mathematically calculated the sum with an 18 percent gratuity. I wondered if this total had crossed Charmin's mind. One of two things would happen shortly. Either he would be the gentleman and understand the tab total due to eating, drinking, and being merry, or he would say, "How in the hell did this happen? It certainly doesn't feel like I ate one hundred dollars. Do you feel like you ate one hundred dollars?" (I'd say, "You started it.")

Dinner was finished and Charmin asked if I would like dessert. I said no since I could barely finish my dinner. Another commandment should read: "Thou shalt not drink three glasses of wine and six glasses of water and expect to have room for more." I was losing track of my commandments from my elementary Carping days, so this may be the fourteenth.

The tab arrived and I was waiting for what, I don't know. Charmin took a look at the itemized bill, put his hands through his hair several times, and adjusted his glasses. He then said, "What the hell is this? This can't be right. There is no way we ate and drank one hundred dollars. You take a look at this."

I did and saw everything was itemized correctly with the addition of an 18 percent gratuity. I brought this to his attention and told him I would pay half the bill. He told me, "No, I am paying the bill but I am going to speak to the owner because this total is wrong." Charmin got up from the table and left. I had no idea what to think or what to do. Sitting and waiting was what I did. This little speed bump had better not screw up the squeezing of the soft stuff, which had been on my mind for the past three weeks.

Charmin returned shortly with no blood on his face, not a big disgrace, and not waving a banner all over the place, so he still must have been friends with Freddy Mercury (the late lead singer of the rock group Queen). In spite of the ending, the evening was fun. I got a chance to see a side of Charmin I had not witnessed with the past two fishings, and I liked it. Observing him in the Freddy mode made me think of positively squeezing the Charmin even more.

Finally, it was time to leave and take the short drive to my house. My mind was on squeezing the Charmin and getting my first kiss. We arrived at my driveway, and Charmin continued with small talk, and then there was a short pause. I was sure this was it; here comes the Charmin, except nothing happened. The pause was too long, so I turned to him and put my arms around his neck and gave him a nice kiss. Not a Frenchy-kind of kiss but just a nice wanting-to-squeeze-the-Charmin kind of kiss. It was the twenty-first century and acceptable for a gal to kiss a guy, I guessed; I guess not. I then told him I had been waiting three weeks for a kiss.

He said, "Really?" just like it never crossed his mind. I was really hoping for a necking fest, but I could see this was not going to happen. I didn't feel stupid, but I did feel disappointed. It's not like I jumped him and demanded sex including whips, chains, handcuffs, and a carpet-cleaning vibrator. I would have waited at least for the fourth date to spring this on him.

Charmin opened the car door and said good-bye, adding that he would call the next week and schedule another dinner date. I guess he considered me his eating companion. He never called. Again, I did not feel stupid, just disappointed. Reflecting and analyzing Charmin,

I questioned whether he may have burped up his one-hundred-dollar meal and drinks on his way home, and it left a bad taste in his mouth, or was it the fact I kissed him and he could not compromise this affectionate gesture with an eating pal? I'll never know.

Epilogue: A year later, I bumped into Charmin at a local grocery store. He looked really nice, like he was going to some kind of outing. His black hair was slicked back, and he looked Charmin hot. I was dressed in a pink striped seer-sucker sundress, flip-flops, tanned as brown sugar, and had not done anything in particular with my short blonde hair. My toddler grandson was seated in the grocery cart. Charmin immediately noticed me and with a big smile said, "Hi." I smiled back and introduced my grandson. He asked how I had been and if I would like to go out to dinner sometime soon. I said dinner would be nice. He said, "Great, I'll call you next week." He never did. I did not feel stupid, and I did not feel disappointed.

As I watched Charmin walk to his car, I made a mental note of the following: Today was the day Charmin left the fishing pond for bigger waters. He was now an honorary graduate, "I'll-Call-You" Carp residing in the hallowed murky waters with bottom feeders. I promised myself to never feel stupid or disappointed when fishing with this species, of which there are many.

My thoughts with regard to graduate status and the "I'll-Call-You" Carp are with not having a skill set including polite conversation offering no commitments; basically, they are cowards. Why can't they just say something like: "I've been busy; I've moved on; I am living in a different state and am home visiting my parents; I got sick on crab cakes and cannot eat any solid food; I beat up a restaurant owner due to an outrageous tab and spent the last year in jail"? Why can't they just say anything besides "I'll call you," when they have no intention of doing so?

In closing, the distinguishing characteristic of Fish versus Carp is what I refer to as their "Gentleman Factor" (or G.F., which should not be confused with G.Q.). A gentleman will either keep his word or, in a polite manner, tell you he enjoyed himself but the sparks or the chemistry was not present. I actually had this happen to me once. I did not feel stupid, but I was disappointed in myself that the Fish could feel my negative energy. In the end, a phone call or some simple words may seem like a small gesture, but in the scheme of things, it is the big gesture distinguishing a Fish from a Carp.

> *Propriety of manners and consideration for others are*
> *the two main characteristics of a gentleman.*
>
> *—Benjamin Disraeli*

Bucky the Tooth

Incoming Carp E-mail: I am a salesman; end of story. The new story is that I am a man with some money, a lover of technology, soccer games, and beverages. The long and short of it is that the only long thing about me is my tooth, so this story will be short.

> *I don't have false teeth. Do you think I'd buy teeth like these?*
>
> —*Carol Burnett*

Introduction: Fresh out of toilet paper, I was on the road again (minus Willy Nelson but the plus is my computer and more marathon online dating, which is now at leg two or 7.4 miles). Fishing around, I hooked Bucky the Tooth. He looked somewhat attractive, sporting a suit and tie and his bio noting sales as his profession. I should have known better, since I am not a sales gal, could not be a sales gal, and will never be a sales gal. It takes a certain kind of person to continually harass someone into buying something they need (and especially if they do not need whatever is being sold). I am not against salespeople; I am just glad I am not one. I prefer online shopping, which provides users with a faceless and nameless shopping cart.

The Novella: I cast Bucky an incoming e-mail, and he took the bait. We decided to meet at the so-called "point of no return" or the notorious bar and grill where my last thoughts were of squeezing toilet paper. In plain English, our fishing site of choice was the same restaurant in which I first met Charmin. My hopes were that the owners of the establishment would see me as a loyal patron and not a hooker.

Meeting Bucky at the bar and grill really took me back, and it was farther than the last pew in church. He looked just like his photo, except for the big front tooth. I could not stop staring at it. I am sure the guy in the movie *The Hangover,* who pulled out his tooth with a pair of pliers over his marriage to Heather Graham, could use it as a replacement. This gives you a visual of his large, economy-size tooth. I know it is not polite to stare at a Fish with a big tooth, but I couldn't help it. It wouldn't have been so bad if he had two big front teeth. I could have then called him Bugs as in Bunny. All the time I was obsessing about Bucky's tooth, Bucky was obsessing about me. I learned this a few minutes later.

Bucky used the word "beverage" and asked if I wanted one. *Webster's Dictionary* defines beverage as a drinkable liquid. Well, I would rather have a glass of wine, and I am pretty sure it is called a cocktail. Who uses a word like beverage? It has to be someone with a big tooth. I wondered how he drank with a tooth resembling a shark's fin without getting it caught on the glass. I guessed I was just going to have to wait and see.

Bucky ordered a beverage, and I ordered a cocktail. We were both doing the once, twice, thrice look me over, not going to work, make the best of it, and next is the new one for the both of us. He does not work for me because he makes poor to little eye contact and has a big tooth. I couldn't even imagine how he kisses, which may be closer to hooking a gal's lip with a fishing lure. I think I did not work for him since I was a little gal dressed casually in a pink nondescript top, beige slacks, with Sketchers on my feet. Maybe he thought since we were meeting at the Phantom of the Opera bar and grill, I would show up in an opera gown sporting cleavage resembling the Mid-Atlantic Ridge. I should introduce Bucky to Lazy. I quickly dismissed this thought, since I was sure Bucky's big tooth would add another gouge to Lazy's already existing ridges and land me in the county jail for an overnighter and breakfast of Froot Loops for endangering a species.

Bucky had his fishing planned in advance, because I was an older gal and figured this out at the time. Actually, anyone could figure this out, even Lazy. During our beverage and cocktail time, Bucky's cell phone rang, and he told me it was important, since it was his son. Well, son of a biscuit! Bucky and the Buckster had a plan. If I wasn't to Bucky's liking, Buckster was to call Daddy Tooth, telling him it was time to pick him up from soccer practice. How lame; he should be fed to the fish at the bottom of the ocean that do not have eyes. Or better yet, feed him to the species of sea urchins that do not have eyes but have eye sensory at the tips of their spines. Maybe the spines are also capable of zapping his big tooth.

With my head bobbing as if cast on rough seas and the big-toothed bottom feeder hitting my line, I nodded my head yes, agreeing that an incoming call from his offspring was understandable. Since I was in the intermediate phase and still had not acquired a will with my spine, I did not have the wherewithal to just get up and leave and hook him with the beverage bill. Bucky was much too strange for me to fret about.

The short of the short story is we do know what repulses or offends others, and we may not have any idea of what is going on in the head of a Carp. Most of the time it is nothing or of little consequence in the big picture of a "Big One," since we are dealing with adult males. I do know with future fishing, when I see a Big Tooth advancing, I am going to ask right up front if he is related to Bucky, and if so, tell him to sacrifice a beverage for a better tooth. If his tooth is anything like Pinocchio's nose and gets longer, it will become his third leg. I wonder how he is going to explain this to his next gal when she is expecting a different kind of third leg.

Epilogue: Bucky was worth poetic prose in that he was a good reality check of what may be going on in each head on a fishing date. Two conversations with Bucky follow, including my rebuttal. It is then up to you to decide which one is fairer in the eyes of Robert Burns and his "best laid plans of mice and men."

*I find that most men would rather have their bellies opened
for five hundred dollars than have a tooth pulled for five.*

—*Martin H. Fischer*

61

He Says, so He Thinks

He says his name is Bucky and he can't stay too long,
What he really is saying is looking at you
is like a bad trip to Hong Kong.

He says he is expecting a very important phone call,
What he really is saying is you are not that important at all.

He says would you like a beverage?
What he really is saying is I hope a "beverage" will kill her courage.

He says I'll have a beer,
What he really is saying is
I'll give her a minute to figure out that away we should steer.

He says he likes you in the color pink with Sketchers on your feet,
What he really is saying is pink is nice but
it would be better as a bra and
stilettos that are not discreet.

He says he has to answer this important phone call,
What he really is saying is yes, son, Buckster is right on the ball.

He says it is his son and he cannot miss this call,
What he really is saying is I love you, son, since
you have rescued me from this pitfall.

He says I have to finish this "beverage" and pick up my son,
What he really is saying is another minute
and I hope this date is done.

He says drink up and I'll walk you to your car,
What he really is saying is I hope you parked in another place afar.

He says out the door and across the street,
What he really is saying is I hope to never
see you again and no repeats.

He says I had a nice time and gives me a big hug,
What he really is saying is I had nicer times wrestling bears in rugs.

He says it is starting to rain and he must run to his car,
What he really is saying is after this date I'm
running straight to the nearest bar.

He shouts back that he had a good time,
What he really is saying is that looks count for everything, every time.

What she says is I am a looker and am mighty fine,
What she really is saying is that I meet these schmucks all the time.

He Says … She Thinks …

He says his name is Bucky and he can't stay too long.
She thinks, thank goodness, since your tooth is way too long.

He says he is expecting an important phone call from his son.
She thinks, thank goodness, since I still can't
get over your *Hangover* tooth, no fun.

He says would you like a beverage?
She thinks, he's checked me out and can see I don't
have Heather Graham's roller skates or cleavage.

He says he'll have a beer.
She thinks, still dwelling, with that tooth, I will have to steer clear.

He says he likes you in the color pink with Sketchers on your feet.
She thinks, nice in pink as in Victoria's Secret would be his sweet.

He says he has to answer this important phone call.
She thinks, thank goodness, I don't know
if he is worth anything at all.

He says it is his son and he needs a ride home
from his practice with soccer,
She thinks, yes, this was all planned in advance
and what a Ben Stiller Focker.

He says I have to pick up my son and finish this "beverage."
She thinks, he can't wait to get out of here
since my breasts aren't full-coverage.

He says drink up and I'll walk you to your car.
She thinks, he would probably rather see me stand in
a corner in a round room with no doors ajar.

He says out the door and across the street.
She thinks, he probably wants me to get hit
in traffic and knocked off my feet.

He says I had a nice time and gives me a big hug.
She thinks, yeah right, with that big tooth
you look like a vampire thug.

He says it is starting to rain and he must run to his car.
She thinks, it really is the both of us who want to run afar.

He shouts back he had a good time.
She thinks, yeah right, and even I don't
believe this for a payment of a dime.

He waves back with a good-bye.
And all the while she thinks, with all his money,
why didn't he fix his teeth, dumb guy?

Boobs

Incoming Carp E-mail: Women typically find me attractive in a Grizzly Adams kind of way, since I sport a beard and big hands that resemble bear paws with claws. I enjoy math problem solving and am a boob man versus long legs and booties that look better on rubber blow-up dolls.

> *The breasts, the hallmark of our culture; you cannot sell anything in America without the breasts.*
>
> *—Phil Donahue*

Preface: The marathon continued, with leg three of the race at 11.1 miles. I am off the hook of Bucky's tooth and ready for the next Fish, who hopefully will be a better storyteller and not a fabricator with an offspring in tow with technology. Even though I have snagged two so far in the marathon race to find the "Big One," I am not twice shy yet nor friends with Ian Hunter at this mile marker. In fact, I am hungry for a man, can almost smell a man, and feel he is not too far in the distance of miles. Jane is sick of chasing Dick around. Yes, they are from the same family, and this does pose a problem.

Introduction: Listening to a man who is a good storyteller is very important when deciding "to fish or not to fish; that is the question." I love storytelling and enjoy someone who also loves word choice, embellishing, dramatic adjectives, and expository writing (not to be confused with suppository writing, which generates from a different source known as speaking from the ass). I found these words from Hamlet: "What a piece of work is man," best suiting this Carp adventure.

Pee Wee Herman and his la la la adventures may help you connect the dots. If not, feel free to connect them yourself.

The Novella: All my *Uno mas no mas* dates came in varying degrees of bizarre, and Big Boob, not his name but fits for this fishing drama, was no exception. At first glance, Big Boob looked like Grizzly Adams from the hit '70s show starring Dan Haggerty. Haggerty and Big Boob sport the same grizzly features, although Dan Haggerty looked more like a soft teddy bear (not to be confused with Charmin) and frequently smiled. Once again, the decision was to meet at a local bar and grill. I had not been to this one for over a month so the stink factor would not be present. Besides, there was a patio area and any possible mackerel fumes could be mistaken for the river area to the west filled with geese droppings.

Big Boob began his storytelling about something that had just happened to him prior to our fishing dinner. His bikes were stolen from the back of his van. They were securely chained, but someone had cut the links with metal cutters. Since this happened prior to our dinner date, he had been scrambling with police reports and was sick in the stomach that such a thing could happen to him. In the end, Big Boob said he would have to replace his bikes, because they were probably dismantled and sold for their pieces. I guess pieces are worth more than the sum of their parts or the whole.

Anyone teaching fractions would love to have this authentic problem in their curriculum. As a former math teacher and lover of numbers, I would certainly use this bike content as a warm-up exercise to properly engage kids. The possibilities are endless when thinking of all the bicycle parts separated and then mixing and matching parts to make different fractional equivalents and then matching the equivalents to different dollar amounts. Besides the endless possibilities, there is the afterthought of how many kids you are encouraging with bike theft.

So storytelling with Big Boob began on a sad note. I tried searching my brain's *Bruce Almighty* file folders for a comparison story so I would be able to make a connection to his pain. I had none, and besides, we had just met. In addition, I had read an article in *Oprah* by Martha Beck with regard to "Emotional Sluts," of which I am truly guilty of more so than less. Emotional sluts feel they must confide something personal when something personal is being shared. She warns us not to do this since it may result in sharing something too personal or embarrassing in nature. After taking many personality tests, I recognize this as a weakness and something I have to work on so as not to succumb to emotional slutting every time a Carp tells me a "woe-is-me" story. Luckily, during this fishing adventure, I pretty much just listened to his storytelling. Any words from me would have distracted him from the scope, sequence, and magnitude of his personal life.

After the bike story, Big Boob continued with another story about his son, who I will call Little Boob, who lived in New Orleans. This storytelling was a work in progress. Little Boob was driving on the Lake Pontchatrain Bridge when all at once, or it may have been more than once, several big waves washed over the guard railings and rolled and smashed cars around like toy cars made in China. American cars would have withstood all the tossing. So Little Boob had a smashed car with no insurance, and Big Boob was pretty sure he was going to get a cell phone call requesting a "Get-Out-of-Jail-Free" card, requiring a rescue costing a few dollars and a few more cents, of which Little Boob has none.

During Big Boob's storytelling, his cell phone does ring, and sure enough, it is Little Boob. It seems the cell phone calls from the Carp in my life thus far have involved offspring. I know from YouTube there is a rock group called Offspring with such hits as "Why Don't You Get a Job" and "The Kids Aren't All Right." It's too bad parents' cell phones do not come equipped with such messages as playback instead of taking the call requiring a bailout without alcoholic beverages, similar to toys in which batteries are not included.

I was hoping he would make the call private by walking to a more discreet area so I would not have to hear the drama, but he did not. The one-sided conversation from Big Boob had him telling Little Boob he was sick and tired of bailing his little thirty-three-year-old boob butt out of binds. The only bailing out of water situations without insurance happened on the *Titanic*. Not knowing the father/son history, this all seemed plausible, and especially with Little Boob's age. It's not like he was thirty and still hadn't been weaned from another boob.

Big Boob hung up the phone, looked at me, and shook his head, then we both shook our heads in agreement. Little Boob will continue to be little boob until the teat is dry. Big Boob blamed all this on his ex-wife. This made perfect sense even though I found myself mentally undressing Big Boob to see if his boobs may be Little Boob's enablers. Since I did not have the courage to ask Big Boob to give me a peep show, we continued with playing "Go Fish."

Storytelling continued with the rest of the story. Big Boob told me Little Boob was bisexual and living in a New Orleans transient community. Not too shocking, yet. Little Boob was supposed to be on his way home from the Big Easy to stand up in his sister's wedding. Not too shocking, yet. Little Boob had no transportation and had to figure out how to get home in time for the wedding. Not too shocking, yet, since people in dire straits usually find a way with their will as long as it still attached to their spine. Little Boob had to be home in time to get a nipple piercing to match his sister's pierced nipple.

This was where I was a little shocked to say the least and had absolutely no emotional-slut connecting words, whatsoever. I have lived a long time and feel I have experienced a diverse life in some measure, but this story was one no one could make up or connect to (I don't think). Either Big Boob is a compulsive liar or his life is really this bizarre. Maybe I am just not as diverse as I once thought and should get out more. I have been out in some respects since I have been to New Orleans several times but only as a heterosexual.

More storytelling continued with the bride, as Daughter Boob, now thirty-one years old and getting married in two weeks. Little Boob is the bridesmaid, since she did not have an even number of matching attendants. Little Boob would be on time for the wedding since Big Boob phoned him while our dinner was being served. He decided to post bail with an extension of auto insurance, a beater car, and time to spare for Little Boob's nipple piercing. It seemed Little Boob's enabler still had a working teat.

My mind had cashed out to the max. I was not even listening to Big Boob as he rambled on and on. I felt the only way I could fit into any part of this conversation was to have a boob job. There was absolutely no way I was getting a nipple piercing. Maybe a tattoo on the boob would be a better fit for me, if tattoos could be considered a fit. Regardless, I still had nothing to say in response since I was definitely not getting a boob job. I like my boobs. With this little set, I will never have to worry about smothering a Carp while he is trying to climax.

Somewhat half listening to Big Boob, I found myself completely digressing with the idea of a pierced-nipple bride and her brother attendant. My mind searched for all the possibilities of haute couture. The only acceptable attire I was able to locate in one of my *Bruce Almighty* file folder drawers was a dress or tuxedo with a peek hole for the piercing. Wedding skirts and pants solo cannot be an option unless they are done tastefully, as in the *Look* magazine 1963 prototype topless bathing suit by the Austrian American Rudy Gernreich. Regardless, the breasts need to be covered. I am sure the Fifteenth Commandment reads, "Thou shalt not show your boobs during the wedding ceremony. Only show your boobs on the honeymoon."

Back to the present, and I realized we were nearly finished with our dinner and Big Boob's storytelling (or maybe it was lying or hallucinating). I loved listening to Big Boob's story. It helped me to understand it is fine to have a somewhat different life and not be able to make a connection. As bizarre as it sounds, Big Boob actually offered me new knowledge. As an educator, I always enjoyed these opportunities. This was one of the few times in my long life I actually sat across the table from a boob and came away with a clear understanding of what one looks like up close and personal. I was confident that there wasn't a college or university that offered required course work called Boob 101, and I felt flattered that I had learned from a master of the art.

Epilogue: Big Boob went in partnership with the rest of the Boobs and wrote a course descriptor and syllabus with tentative schedule for Boob 101. The prerequisite is any student applying must be engaged or planning to be married and have a fetish for multiple piercings.

Great boobs trump stupid words.

—*Mental Poo merchandise*

Shame, Shame, Shame ... Shame of Fools

Incoming Carp E-mail: I am politically inclined and experienced in public office. A gal of interest would be one who likes to discuss money, parking agreements, and the incompatibility with regard to technology. Also, I am about bravado and do not consider it a shameless act.

> *Time shall unfold what plighted cunning hides:*
> *Who cover faults, at last shame them derides.*
>
> —*William Shakespeare,* King Lear

Introduction: One evening, I received an e-mail from a Fish who said he liked my picture and my biography and asked if I was interested in fishing. I was now on leg four, or 14.8 miles of my marathon summer, and had only responded with Fish who had photos. There was no picture included with his note, so I replied, "No, I do not fish with those who do not have a license," which meant a picture must be included. He replied he didn't have any pictures, nor did he have a camera. No hook for this Fish, and I tell him to keep fishing.

The Novella: I continued to receive a number of e-mails from this Fish who I will refer to as No Shame Carp, explaining he finally found a friend who could take his picture and upload it to the fishing site. At this point, I said fine, but had no idea why. I still had a difficult time being upfront and saying what I should when it comes to matters of the heart when it should be the other way around. When my heart is in danger of being invaded by a Carp, I should know better. After many Carp adventures, I do know a little better but am still not there by any

71

means. Carp come in various sizes and shapes, and have the ability to mutate. Therefore, figuring out Carp is not a true science.

No Shame Carp's photo indicated he was somewhat attractive in the older gray-haired sense and had a nice smile. Also, it showed him from the waist up; thank goodness it is not a head shot. His attire was a sweatshirt with the logo "Replacement Parts." The logo in itself was interesting; I began to wonder what parts were being replaced since no other words were accompanied. On the wall, in the background, were pictures of speed boats, so I thought the replacement parts may have been for boats rather than my other line of thought, which was about body parts.

He appeared a little heavy, but many older men who are overweight can still pull it off. Why is it that men can pull this off? Why do we allow them to think that a little pork on the belly is fine, love handles are a sign of love, and flapping-in-the-breeze butts make them look skinny from the backside? This is a double standard. Regardless of the double standards and the digression, which can push me off the deep end, I continued to reply to No Shame Carp's fishing.

We talked on the cell phone and made a date for that night to meet at my favorite bar and grill. Eventually, I may be banned from all bars in my area, since I will be known for bringing in stinking Carp. Most fine establishments should post, "No shoes, no shirt, no Carp, no eat." In doing so, this may eliminate eateries of choice and my penchant for dating Carp.

Up Close and Personal with meeting (and not staring at Robert Redford), I saw No Shame's face matched his photo; this was from the waist up and included his logo "Replacement Parts" sweatshirt. Either he had a bounty on the sweatshirts or he hadn't changed his clothing since the picture was taken by his friend. From the waist down, it was a different story since he had on a pair of plaid cargo shorts, tube socks, and an odd pair of sneakers with heels labeled Jack Rabbits. I wondered who dressed him for the part of Rodney Dangerfield from the movie *Caddy Shack*.

No Shame Carp definitely had no sense of style in addition to no camera and uploading sense. Maybe he was a "problem child" and related to Bon Scott of AC-DC fame. I have seen both Bon Scott and No Shame in a pair of shorts, and the difference was that Bon Scott's shorts came with a visible package. It is next to impossible to advertise a package when wearing a pair of cargo shorts. I resigned myself to another evening of smiling, head bobbing, and drinking wine. My motto at this point in my fishing career was "No wine, no dine on your time." This motto will never change, since I do not plan to stop drinking at any point in my future fishing career.

During head bobbing, No Shame Carp told me he was a public official who made no money and was in this profession because he loved politics. Looking at his attire, he could have fooled me about being a public official, but the no money made perfect sense. I, on the other hand, do not have a vested interest in politics and find more enjoyment writing a lot of bad words acquired from fishing with Fockers and donkeys (this is the polite way of saying expletives and getting away with foul language).

I digress once again with *Oprah* (November 2010) and Elizabeth Banks (page 52) in which she states her best virtue: "A wicked mouth. And the best virtue is prudence in using it. Ladies should use F-bombs sparingly but to great effort." I love it! Elizabeth has given me permission to use the F-bomb. I won't say it here, but "trust me" (and I am not related to Richard Nixon), I will be using the F-bomb soon. Carp just push me off the deep end, especially if they are public officials who may have the same running record as a "problem child."

Before-dinner conversation continued with public office chatter, none of which mattered. No Shame Carp told me he loved the work because he was fond of the public figure imagine. Public figures get to be in the limelight, wear a suit and tie, and wear foolhardy clothing when off duty, and they are given the so-called privilege of never having to shut up or show how many teeth they have left. He continued with bringing up the nonsalaried issue and said he should decide on another profession with a more lucrative outcome. It seemed strange an older fella was still trying to figure out what he wanted to be when he grew up.

No Shame Carp told me he had an ex-wife but did not defer to her for the lack of money. All his lack of money and issues were his doing, since he couldn't find the right lure to hook or shut his flapping public office lips. I think he mentioned he made about ten thousand dollars a year, and this money was spent on his parking space emblazoned with his name.

The conversation changed to my side of the table. No Shame Carp asked me about my work and accomplishments. I should have just shut my mouth and stated I worked in public service, and be firm with the fact I am private with first-time Fish. Instead, I pulled out the biggest lure in the tackle box, which was definitely the wrong one for this Carp. I told him exactly what I did as a life passion and did not leave out any of my accomplishments and awards. My life is a litany of rightly deserved deeds. I was not sure if this was a blonde or *Sarah Plain and Tall* stupid moment, but either way I could hear Forrest Gump saying to me, "Stupid is as stupid does." Momma would not have supported me during this moment of emotional slutism.

Sitting across from me, No Shame Carp was completely stupefied for a moment, but only for a moment. He quickly found control of his rubbery lips and began gushing like Old Faithful in Yellowstone Park. His gushing did not come in forty-five-minute intervals but in forty-five-second sparks. Gush, gusher, gushing, and the following was emitted with no omissions: "Oh my gosh, I am sitting with a celebrity! You are amazing! I am just blown away! I want to see you on a permanent basis! We should be lovers! I can't stop looking at your face! I can get a better apartment! I own many boats and have a franchise that sells sweatshirts with the logo 'Replacement Parts.' I promise to find work that doesn't involve politics! You can have my parking space. You are a keeper, as in a twelve-inch large mouth bass. Wow, wow, wow!" It is amazing to experience whiplash when the effect has not been produced during an auto accident.

Still blasting and gushing away, our dinner of fish and chips was served with drinks; yes, I was drinking wine and he was drinking a Coke. I truly don't remember eating but I do remember looking around and feeling totally embarrassed sitting across from this whole lot of ass. There wasn't a big enough donkey on the face of the earth to carry his carcass full of crap. No Shame Carp truly was an animal in himself and most likely was his own beast of burden, definitely not related to Mick Jagger of Rolling Stones fame.

Fun times always have to end, and this one was no different. It was at this time, No Shame Carp decided to show his true Carp status.

He pulled out a ten-dollar bill from of his pocket and told me it was all the money he had and asked if I could pay my portion of the bill. I wondered if he kept his driver's license in his underwear, since he didn't appear to be wearing a man bra. Instead of feeling sorry for him, since he is a public official without money but is allowed to wear cargo shorts and tube socks, I now realized that he was shameless. How can someone gush over me nonstop like I am the best thing since calamari and ahi tuna and not come prepared to pick up the tab? It seemed he would be mortified, but instead this seemed to be his normal behavior.

I told him yes, I had my own money, but I should have added as a public official, he probably could pick up the tab and deduct the expenditure from his taxes. Maybe public officials do not pay taxes so this information would not be a part of his so-called knowledge bank, which is not to be confused with banking institutions such as City Bank.

We got up to leave, and yes he walked me to my car and gushed the entire way. Bile and saliva were forming in my mouth, and I knew I was going to puke and it was still daylight. Fifteen minutes from home, I was thinking of the ice cold bottle of German Riesling in my refrigerator. No detox for this gal after this shameless ten-dollar event.

No sooner did I get home when my cell phone rang. I saw it was No Shame Carp's number and did not pick up the call and let the message go to voice mail. What a plankton I was to give No Shame Carp my cell phone number. His message was a replica of his one-sided gushing drama at the bar and grill. He went on and on about how wonderful I was, wanted to see me again, how refreshing I was, how wow, wow, wow (and those are his exact number of wows, it may have been more), and just went overboard like a drunken sailor without his shoes.

I deleted the phone message, turned on my computer, and immediately went to the fishing site to block him from all future fishing. The rest of the evening was spent sitting on my dock by the so-called bay, listening to Otis Redding, drinking good Riesling wine, swishing my feet in the water, and relishing the little minnows and blue gills nipping at my toes. Life is good when you swim with the right Fish.

Epilogue: A few weeks later while TV channel surfing, I saw none other than No Shame Carp on the fishing channel. It seemed

Replacement Parts paid for advertising space during the programming, and No Shame Carp, as spokesperson gusher personified, sang about replacing a number of boat items including adhesives and sealants, anchors, bimini tops, fuel accessories, fenders and buoys, hatches, and antennas, just to name a few. Finally, instead of ending with a catchy Replacement Parts ditty, I heard AC/DC background music and lyrics to: "I'm a Problem Child." Do problem children end up on the highway of endless commercials, or do they end up in hell as Carp luring customers to buy replacement parts? There isn't an answer to this question; just jeopardy.

Shame is an ornament to the young; a disgrace to the old.

—Aristotle

Zealously Is Misery

I want you to like me,
But remember this is the first time we have met.
Who says such a thing?
Already thinking I am in regret.

You know I am religious,
Even though I have never practiced my faith.
I want to go back to the church,
And remember, we haven't even had a date.

I went to your high school and am older than you.
Then why can't I find you in any of the yearbooks,
And why doesn't anyone even know you?
Not even students, football players, and no others do.

Do you want to go out to dinner?
This is the fourth call this week.
Since the zealot is retired,
With time on his hands with this he does speak.

Phone call, phone call, and more endless chatter,
His interest and note taking is his matter,
Trying to find out everything and not missing a detail,
And what you are finding out about him all seems to fail.

He drinks draft beer and it is wine you like,
The German, the Riesling is of his dislike.
He says he will try some and study the grape,
Become cultured and investigating everything about your shape.

Oh yes, I live with guys in a rented trailer for fun,
Who are in their twenties and this one is sixty-one.
I lost all of my money to multiple wives with multiple kids.
The message is becoming clearer,
The zealot is looking for a place to live.

Entering, smelling of draft beer, stale cigarettes and chew,
His eyes open wide with my house as his view.
Thoughts are searching, is he looking for a weekend honey dew?
My take is his house is a hovel and a guys' pad for a few.

I'll pick you up at 8:00 p.m. on Friday,
No wait, I will call to set the date.
Two days of thinking, is this my fate?
It is the zealot speaking,
I want everything about you,
I want you to like me,
And remember, I just met you.

Friday comes with cell phone in hand,
Hoping voice mail picks up at my command.
Yippee, a voice mail and this is what I said,
"Thank you for asking me on a dinner date,
But I have decided to pass,
For in your effort to be the zealot,
You have crucified yourself with your past."

Zealots give themselves away in their zeal,
And in thinking more than twice, they have no appeal.
Their motives, they think are pure, for they know no other way,
But in their zeal, my desire fades away.

The zealot imagines himself as someone
dying to give attention and affection.
But in the end, it is your stuff that is his motivation.
Once he enters smelling of draft beer, stale cigarettes and chew,
It is time to send him back in time and say adieu.

Oxy

Incoming Carp E-mail: I am a man of small means and love the simple apartment life. I quit smoking cigarettes a month ago. This is quite an accomplishment since I began this wonderful habit at the age of ten and am now fifty-five. My father gave me my first cigarette in the guise of a tampon with explicit directions to deliver it to my older sister, who has the habit seven days out of every month. He was embarrassed to do so, and my mother could not come to terms with someone else besides her having a period, having sex, and may soon be having babies.

A man can be short and dumpy and getting bald
but if he has fire, women will like him.

—*Mae West*

Introduction: I was now on leg five, which equated to 18.5 miles of my marathon summer of fishing with no "Big One" in the net. It surprised me that I still had a positive attitude since the last four events brought prizes with surprises and a barrel almost full with bottom feeders. I wondered if the fumes from Carp act much like snorting cocaine, thus my continuing smiles and laughter with fishing. I had never had cocaine, so the closest connection is laughing gas or nitrous acid (or maybe it is nitrous oxide). I just know that when I had a dose of it during a yanking of my lower wisdom teeth, the dentist had to restrain me since I was constantly trying to get up and find John Cougar Mellencamp and his woman who wouldn't drive him crazy. To this day, I cannot listen to the song without bursting out laughing. The laughter must be through osmosis since I do not have a container of nitrous oxide at home, although I sure would like to have a suck of the stuff once in a while. It would help me through the times of meeting Carp who drove me crazy (and still do).

The Cliff Notes Version: Of all the Carp I have met, Oxy, which is short for Oxymoron, since he is an adult male and Carp fodder related to my past experiences, was one of the most memorable. Even though he definitely was a Carp, his stories, which involved detailed summaries of his "hot, damn hots," provided me with an experience with one of life's contradictions. I still haven't decided if he was an Oxy (related to the Oxydol Cleaning Soap magnate) or a Moron, due to his pompous importance with regard to his "manhood." Either way, this Carp was definitely on fire. Mae West assures women that they would still like him; it just didn't happen to be me.

Oxy was a good Carp in that he was a gentleman and picked up the tab for our dinner, which included the jumbo shrimp appetizer and gourmet pizza topped with vegetarian meatballs, served with smooth whiskey and the bonus of a free gift coupon for our next visit. He never once made me feel uncomfortable with the menu and pricing and lavished me with three glasses of good German Riesling wine, since I cannot handle smooth whiskey. It may have been four glasses, since I did not have dessert. Oxy ordered dessert, choosing the pound cake, which weighed twelve ounces and was 99 percent fat-free topped with sweet and sour strawberries.

The Novella: Oxy sent me an e-mail expressing interest with our similar likes with regard to music. Since we were both teenagers during the 1960s, our favorites included classic rock and soul. Led Zeppelin, the Temptations, Smokey Robinson and the Miracles, and of course the Beatles were the darts that hit the easy target of connections. Also, we both enjoyed going out for dinner, drinks, and fun. Oxy told me he quit smoking a long time ago, whatever that means. What someone did for the past fifty years or so did not bother me (unless it was life threatening, such as coming to the table with a butcher knife, stun gun, or cattle prod. Stun guns are definitely a subject during a second date. Cattle prods are third date conversations with therapy as the follow-up.).

Oxy and I decided to meet at the bar and grill, the same one on the river that disguised the stink factor of incoming Carp with the warm smells of sulfur and geese droppings. In his e-mails, he warned me from the outset that he loved to talk and talk a lot, much like silent women. This was an understatement. I don't think I said more than a dozen words during the evening other than, "Yes, I'll have another glass of wine." Now that I reevaluate the word count, I did say twenty-eight words I am aware of, since I had four glasses of wine. This was my stance when I resolve to another evening with another Carp who is going to tell me a lot of crap.

I digress. This cycle of just hooking Carp is unending. The reality is I love to play dress-up. My closets are full of free shipping from Victoria's Secret, J. C. Penney, and Macys.com. I am the queen of many things, and one of them is free shipping. I can also be "Queen for a Day." If you are my age or close, you will know what this means. If you don't, just be a queen for a day and pretend you are Paris Hilton, who has a master of arts in the field. I actually like Paris Hilton. She is a reality check of what life would be like if I didn't have aspirations and wasn't interested in suppository writing and a blind spot for meeting a whole lot of asses, rather than expository writing, which involves just ass holes. Blind ambition is better than no ambition.

Head bobbing began with Oxy's storytelling, fibbing, or maybe it was hallucinating about his ideal home, which was an apartment. With one long sentence, he explained he had no furniture except for a folding table, chairs, TV, and his bed; his life was much less complicated since there was no lawn to cut, no snow to shovel, not much maintenance, and not much space. Entertaining was quite limited since most gals do not choose to party in the parking lot. The choices for sexual entertainment are the bed, the table, or the floor. Even men of means may only have these to offer since tables, beds, and floors can be distinguished with both means. Low means the floor with linoleum, and high means the floor with ceramic costing more than five dollars a tile. Both floorings are hard, so there really isn't any difference with flooring as a sexual preference.

Oxy continued with little slips, and they were not the kind one has when a shoe slides on a Polish blow, requiring pinching of the nose with a thumb and index finger and blowing, since Kleenex is not available (this knowledge is one of the godsends of having a grandson). The first slip was with regard to his fetish with cleanliness, which is close to godliness. This didn't surprise me, since he was dressed very well in a suit and tie, the little hair that he had was in place, and his fingernails were clean and well groomed. I once had a male colleague tell me gals can always tell how clean a guy really is by his shoes. Shoes tell the entire story of a Carp's walking that should accompany his talking. Everything else can go to pot, with the exception of the shoes. Shoes must be expensive and clean. I took a quick look under the table, and the shoes were clean and good to go. Even Carrie Bradshaw knows it is the shoes that are the distinguishing factor of a Big versus a Carp. At this stage of my dating career, I cannot handle a Carp with crappy shoes who is not well groomed.

The second slip was the slip of his tongue, which resembled head cheese. I rehearsed this night over and over again and do not even remember the first fifteen minutes. Oxy talked and talked and talked, and the feeling was another experience with whiplash associated with injuries from a car wreck. Next time a guy tells me he likes to talk a lot, I am going to come prepared with a neck brace so I can at least remember the first fifteen minutes. I am sure there was some good stuff to remember that would add to this story, but the only thing I can remember is the kink in my neck.

The third slip told me he had absolutely no money. Why on earth do butt-head Carp introduce themselves by, "Hi, I might be glad to meet you, and I have no money"? I was taught by the powers that be (who are my grandsons) that money is not a topic of conversation. Never discuss religion, politics, and money. They are a surefire indication of an argument on the horizon and "give me back my bullets" is a part of the package. Lynyrd Skynyrd holds the purse to my bullets.

I always understood not talking about religion and politics, because they are no-win topics based on opinions, but discussing money is just *Sarah Plain and Tall* stupid. At this point, I am only concerned if the Carp can pick up the tab and has a little more than ten dollars, since I hover in the twenty-dollar range with concerns of a liquid diet. Also, since I am once again in the prostitute stance, I expect to be paid for my efforts with regard to listening.

Very soon, the slips were getting serious, and incessant chatter from his side of the table tallied the number of women he had asked to his apartment. As a math gal, I was piqued with interest and wondered if

I could use this information in a problem-solving group task with my students. More importantly, I needed to listen to the data represented from the tallies to understand if it translated into a bar, pie, or pictograph. In my little head, the cloud spelled out the next best seller, and it will be entitled *Math Problem Solving for Smarties.*

My head was full of clouds of problems as he continued with womanizing, sex-capades, and rapid movement of rubbery carp-like lips. Every Carp I had met thus far had full fleshy lips that flapped a mile a minute. If I were to take a stopwatch to his mouth, I am sure I could clock his incessant chatter at under the four-minute mile. My other thoughts circled back to the OK Corral, with regard to possible storytelling, fibbing, or hallucinating. If anyone was hallucinating now, it was me. Psychedelics and mushrooms might be a side I will consider in lieu of the jumbo shrimp appetizer. I was pretty sure they did not serve nitrous oxide.

More little stories continued, including one about his manhood, which was certainly in reference to his penis. Oxy was in the group of men who are over the age of fifty, and their eleventh commandment reads, "The Frito Bandito never loses his libido." The twelfth commandment reads, "When Frito loses his libido, Viagra comes to the rescue." All men are about their manhood, but men over fifty are more so due to the fact their biological clock is ticking, and they don't know when they may have to resort to self-medicating.

I have no idea why some men are opposed to drugs. If I had not received the Salk vaccine for polio, I may have been a cripple or confined to a wheelchair. I'll make sure I add this detailed summary for the next fellow who has trouble with his penis standing up straight. I like standing up straight.

Oxy told me he was a "real man" and not a victim of circumstances of numb sensations, at least not yet. Therefore, poking and prodding was his agenda of fuzzy logic. He proclaimed that he forbade the ornament that is dearest to his heart and closest to his groin to become the center of affliction. He told me all this with a straight face, and my face appeared even straighter, resembling a line of symmetry. I continued to be amazed at what men share on a first date. It may sound strange that I had to live so long before I actually met an all-out braggart, but my general thoughts with men and their interest level was to just get down to business, with showing and telling afterwards. Maybe these guys never got their turn in kindergarten.

Dinner was served with more information about Oxy's penis, or as he referred to it, his "manhood" ("boyfriend" seemed more appropriate, since he was definitely an adult male). Maybe he thought the word was more polite, endearing, or the next best thing to affordable housing with regard to his virility, but the fact of the matter is he was still talking about his penis. He told me impotence was incomprehensible. Therefore, as long as his manhood was able to salute to attention, he was going to keep looking for fresh pork to poke. Obviously, he had not heard of the Privacy Act required with first dates. Maybe I should have told him to go to the bathroom first before we started this date so he could use a clean toilet and empty his mouth before he washed his hands.

Oxy continued to spill his guts, much like chum being thrown to attract giant marlin. He described a date with a woman he was absolutely nuts about; she really made the sparks fly, and the chemistry made him wish he would have paid more attention to the subject in high school. His exact words were, "She was hot, damn hot," as if he was expecting me to share a similar experience and become his emotional slut. More explicitly, "She was hot, damn hot, damn hot, damn hot!" I wondered how many hots make a damn hot? How many hots make a dame hot? Robin Williams found the answer to damn hot in the jungles of Vietnam. Maybe I should have suggested to Oxy that he could find all the damn hots he wanted in a tropical rain forest.

Oxy had no room in his pea brain to understand the sisterhood. Chickens probably had more colored matter than he, and they also come with breasts for fondling. I am not sure what color a chicken's brain is, but I am sure Oxy's was not gray. I came to the conclusion he was a species of Carp that cannot be taught to swim upstream. Nothing I say will ever matter or will change the color of his matter, and all this definitely made him another bottom feeder and eligible for extra coupons for chum at Long John Silvers.

For normal Carp, there is no new normal. Carp don't change. The only thing worth changing is their dinner partners. I hope for his sake the stiff member of his family of one remains alert. Heaven forbid, I read in tomorrow's obituary that Oxy was among the first who died of complications of manhood afflictions due to lack of drugs and regular visits to a mosquito-infested tropical rain forest.

Before we parted, Oxy pulled out a cigarette from his breast pocket (this was before smoking was banned from all eateries) and lit it. I was surprised but not really, since he did request seating in the smoking area and smelled of cigarette smoke when we first met. I did not think too much of this since he just finished citing me the Book of Revelations according to the Acts of Penis, and this may have been his after-sex smoke from a previous hot damn. I commented about the smoking and thought he had quit some time ago, whatever that means. He said he tried but told me he was not good with commitments. Aye, now we have another revelation from the Acts of Relationships. Why didn't he just offer this nugget from the outset and we could have parted like the waters in the Red Sea? I could refer him to a gal at the Local Smoke and Choke for his next "hot damn."

We finished with dinner and my bladder was floating. I did not even want to take the time to use the clean toilet. My car was parked a block away, but I assured Oxy I could make the walk by myself. Of course, he would not hear of this. He paid the tab and wanted to make sure he stayed true to his idea of a gentleman, and I stayed true to being his prostitute. This so-called kind gesture took another half hour of my time. His final words still were talking about hot, damn hot.

When replaying this night over, I thought Oxy saw me as a therapist. Maybe because I am an educator, he saw me as a Dr. Melfi of sorts. I guess I'll have to ask Tony Soprano what he thinks about this manhood deal, or maybe ordeal, I just put myself through. Tony will probably advise that Oxy needs to be a real man and just say the word "penis." What kind of a badda bing badda boom calls a penis a manhood?

Epilogue: Another day, another Carp, and still no "Big One." I wondered if I would ever be someone's "hot damn." I wondered if someone would give a damn if I am hot. I wondered if it had to be hot in order for me to give a damn; how about I don't give a broad hot damn? Now there was an interesting concept; a broad how damn or is it broad hot dam? I wondered if it was located on the Dong Nai River system in Vietnam. I have nothing else of importance or interest to say.

> *"Only when manhood is dead—and it will perish*
> *when ravaged femininity no longer sustains it—only*
> *then will we know what it is to be free."*
>
> —*Andrea Dworkin*

Here is a list of Oxy's favorite morons: adult male, boyfriend, quit smoking, clean toilet, authentic replica, silent woman, affordable housing, free gift, numb sensation, detailed summary, dead drunk, smooth whiskey, jumbo shrimp, alone in a crowd, gourmet pizza, twelve-ounce pound cake, 99 percent fat free, fuzzy logic, vegetarian meatballs, and butt-head. Can you think of others?

Mayo

Incoming Carp E-mail: I believe I am handsome, thin, athletic, well traveled, with a past as my real present. I have not changed. It is merely your interpretation of what is real. My favorite condiment is mayo and I only use a tablespoon.

> *Gentiles are people who eat mayonnaise for no reason.*
> —*Robin Williams*

Introduction: Aggressive Aquarium Fish—Tiger Barb. While the Tiger Barb is usually a good community aquarium fish, it has a reputation as a fin nipper if not content. Tiger Barbs have wide golden bodies with bold black tiger stripes and reddish fins and tail. They prefer to be in a school with a lot of space. Since they are prone to nipping fins, they should not be kept with angelfish or other long-finned fish.

I offer this information as to where I am in my head with regard to my summer of love and fishing. With leg six and another 3.7 miles to add before I reach a total of 22.2, I am still positive, polite, and as friendly as Shirley Temple and Kelly Ripa in one package, but my insides are changing, and I am feeling a little bolder from the experience of the past rod and reel casts. I feel like a Tiger Barb in that if the next Carp is not the so-called "Big One," I am going to nip his fins and feed him to the "hot damn" that sings back-up to Justin Timberlake's "Lovestoned: I Think She Knows."

Preface: One of the most frustrating fishing events involved Carp who post pictures that are not current. I have met many Carp who do not even remotely resemble the photos accompanying their biographies. Many of the pictures are outdated, meaning at one time, the Carp had a full head of hair, was trim and slim, was actually handsome, and from the background may have traveled. The foreground is a disguise of their present in-body and ultra-ego state.

The Novella: I love mayonnaise, alias mayo, especially if it is mixed with olive oil. So, when an e-mail came from a Fish, which I will refer to as Mayo, wanting to meet me over something mixed with mayo, this sounded like fun with someone who may actually have a great sense of humor. Also, Richard Gere played the part of Zack Mayo in the movie *An Officer and a Gentleman.* Since 1982, I have been enamored with mayo and Gere as Mayo. My Mayo and I decided to meet, at (what else?) a bar and grill, and order something served with mayo.

Arriving on time in my trendy capris, cropped matching blouse, and hair longer than I like since I did not have time to make an appointment for a hair cut, I found myself in the waiting mode. I did not see Mayo anywhere, so I decided to check out the wine shop. The cashier recognized me from previous fishing and smiled. I was trying to remember the last time I was there with a Carp and began sniffing the area for fumes. No smell, no telltale odor, and no bones still lying on the floor, so it was fine to let a new Fish into this pond.

Bored and not in the mood to buy wine, I decided to go back to the lobby and wait. After fifteen minutes, I decided to give this Fish fifteen more minutes as a "Get-Out-of-Jail-Free" card. Fifteen minutes later, in greased Mayo as if the open door was the entry way for sliding on Mazola on a swimming mat. He was so upset with regard to his lateness, he actually slid in through the front door. He stared down at me wearing shorts, was round of body, had greased-down mayo (not to be confused with slick-backed) hair covered with a baseball cap, huge sunglasses, and a pull-over parka. Mayo looked nothing like his posted photo. I stared back, looking for any connection with regard to resemblance. I saw nothing.

Mayo explained his tardiness was due to not giving himself enough time to squeeze in both his bingo game and vet appointment for his pooch. He continued by telling me that he was retired and spent all his time traveling the church circuit as the local bingo champ. Poochy had recurrent bouts of mange and dug his sores when not receiving the proper medication. These were the magic two of his life, and he was looking for a magic three, which may be me.

Bingo is not high on my list; in fact, it is not on my list at all. I prefer rowdy entertainment, and the only rowdy I see with bingo are the balls spinning around in the rotating wheel of chance, which Mayo may consider his wheel of fortune. Bingo? Egads! Well, here I go again. Shoulda, coulda, woulda walked out but a dinner served with mayo and Mayo somehow seemed entertaining.

The receptionist seated us at a table on the outside deck. Next, the litany of questions and answers; hopeful we would connect on a topic of interest and become emotional sluts. Mayo looked at me and asked why I would be interested in a much older Fish. I explained it was not about the age but what one does with the age. Five years either way can make or break the experience, depending on health, appearance, chemistry, and emotional stability. Finances were a biggie too. I don't say this, but it is always on my mind. I can take care of myself, and I am not about to take care of someone else hook, line, and sinker. I am not an enabler. Enabling is for boobs.

I was dying to ask him about the picture posted on the online site but decided this was a bad move early on. I was not getting any better with regard to *Up Close and Personal* and prayed for saving grace. I will soon be able to be graceless and just ask the "to die for" questions and put both of us out of our misery. When is losing my manners going to be a good option? I would love to just say, "Your photo does not match your real self, so this self is not getting *Up Close and Personal*. For that exercise with intimacy, you will have to enlist the efforts of Michelle Pfeiffer and play the part of Robert Redford."

We continued our small talk with the topic of bingo. I told him I only played organizational bingo once and was not a good sit-down kind of gal, unless it involved my riding lawn mower. Mayo, on the flip side, was a sit-down kind of guy who definitely was skilled in the area of incessant chatter. I had moved from "hot damn" to "I don't give a damn" about sitting and playing bingo.

I listened to twenty minutes of the layout of the diocese of Catholic churches sponsoring bingo events and the fact he doesn't even use a GPS to travel the circuit with his Forty Mule Team and Borax vehicle as mode of transportation; for you younger guys and dolls, imagine the big hotdog vehicle used in *Dumb and Dumber*. It seems taking the bus would be cheaper, but money may not be an issue since he was the chump of champs; this is exactly how he described himself with a smile from one side of his greased hair above the ear to the other. I am glad he wore a billed cap and decided to keep it on; usually this is *Sarah Plain and Tall* stupid manners, but letting him slide on this one was better than seeing how much Mazola was on the top of his head.

Mayo decided to take a breath, looked at me, told me I had very beautiful green eyes (even with my pink glasses), and then dropped a bomb that was bigger than a fart escaping from Woodcock's pants. He told me he had never run, will never run, and the closest he will get to running is a run to the bathroom during bingo intermission. Whoever thought of intermission during a bingo event? No one is exercising anything but their thumb and index finger, and what do they have to do with urination? Again, I digress but come back to reality with my thoughts on running and my passion for the choice including the three h's: heart, health, and hips, which he certainly did not practice.

The Cliff Notes version is that running is a private, solo effort; it does not involve an intermission (unless you count stopping off the road for a pee, in which you do not have to wait in line) but does include drugs in the form of endorphins, as in a drunken euphoric stupor at about the two-mile marker of my six-mile run. I would never expect someone to run with me, nor would I want the company; panting alongside of me, looking at a watch, smelling Ben-Gay and stinking man sweat, having farts slip out and possibly a little residual, and making meaningless conversation are all Thou Shalt Nots on my list of commandments.

In my head, I am rehearsing: bingo, sit down; running, stand up, much like my two-year-old grandson, who tells people out loud what they are supposed to do during a church service. I learned to never put his jacket on too soon because then he tells the parishioners it is time to go before the priest has given the final blessing. I am blest.

We then move onto the next fart: my hair. I thought I was the only one who thought I had Carrie Bradshaw big hair, but according to Mayo, my hair was huge as in enormous, gigantic, and most of all vast. As funny as it was, Mayo next told me to turn around so he could see if the back matched the front and the sides. I was not offended and told him so. I pick my offenses, and one of the number ones is running, and we were past this. I told him it's not that I had a lot of hair, it's just what I do have, I have a lot of; meaning a lot of thin, fine hair. It's like someone telling you they are big-boned when they are short and are carrying too much weight.

Enough small chatter and head bobbing; the waitress made herself known to take our orders. Mayo said he'd have the crab cakes and a Coke. He told me he was going to order dinner and a couple of drinks but decided to change his mind. As of this moment, he was now on a diet and had quit drinking. What the hell was this not eating and drinking? I lived for drinking, and especially lots of wine on a frequent basis. It took me my entire life to build up the stamina, and I was not going to go through withdrawal for something I enjoy with someone who decided to have an epiphany. This was not an "Oh well, what the hell" kind of moment, so I ordered the crab cakes and a glass of white Zinfandel.

I asked Mayo what made him decide to make this life-altering commitment on our first, and it will be our last, fishing date. He said I was an inspiration to a better lifestyle and possibly a new image. I looked at him and wondered if a new image included not wearing a cap and using Goo Be Gone to get the Mazola out of his hair.

The crab cakes arrived and were the appetizer, not the entrée. They were served on a tiny, tiny plate meant for a munchkin and were each the size of a tablespoon (minus the table). There were only two on the munchkin plate, and this was definitely not enough to feed a hungry little gal who had run six miles earlier in the day. I sat and stared at the two globs of mushy mayo. I ate my plops, drank my wine, and ordered a second glass with thoughts of the last supper of a convicted criminal including meat, potatoes, and dessert with Godiva chocolates. Mayo ate his small plops, drank his Coke, and celebrated his first diet meal and diet drink. I looked around for a potential drinking partner. No one else was eating on the deck, and I was doomed to return my eyes to Mazola Boy.

We parted for the evening, with his final words telling me he would call once he reviewed his map of the diocese with upcoming organizational bingo events. Bradley Cooper and *The Hangover* play in my mind: "That's not gonna happen." I don't own a Forty Mule Team and Borax vehicle and am not going to round up any little doggies to plant my butt in a seat with the Bingo Chumpion. I was so disheartened over the tablespoon of mayo (minus the table) that our parting only involved watching him take off in his purple Eldorado, which must have been colored by *Harold and His Purple Crayon*. My last thought on the way home was I forgot to bite off his greased haired fins as a Tiger Barb would do and add them to his crab with mayo for extra flavor.

A few days later, Mayo called and greeted me with, "Hi, doll!" There was silence on my end and what conversation was emitted was very stiff; I cannot lie, and my face shows, even over the telephone. He came right out and said it like all grown-ups should. He told me he sensed something was different. He said, "Is there something I should know about?"

I now took the stance of a Tiger Barb and said, "Yes, you don't even look like your picture! It's not about the bingo, the Mazola in your hair instead of in the salad, or that you drive a Forty Mule Team with Borax vehicle to get from one part of the diocese to the other. Did you actually forget to wear glasses and picked the wrong photo to upload to the fishing site? I could maybe come to terms with that but a photo under false pretenses is something I cannot get past. It is like ordering an online acupuncture ring for your ear as a diet device and receiving a rubber band instead." I then said good-bye and was sure I just blew all the Mazola off the top of his head of hair minus the cap. For once, I became a Tiger Barb and wondered if I would have the stamina to keep up the momentum.

Epilogue: This fishing event saddens me to this day. I am not dwelling on it by any means, but I do think of him and how things may have ended differently with a sincere representation from the outset. I once e-mailed a Carp who had posted a baby photo. I asked him what that was all about. He said he thought it was a good way to get women interested since the baby photo was so endearing. He confessed he had never been married nor had any children. I wondered in what Book of Revelations he found the guiding words expressing that a baby picture was the ultimate catch for a gal and ensured procreativity. Obviously, there isn't one since he is still single and without children.

My favorite sandwich is peanut butter, baloney, cheddar cheese, lettuce, and mayonnaise on toasted bread with catsup on the side.

—*Hubert H. Humphrey*
(former Senator from Minnesota)

The Invisible Man

Tell me about yourself or
Better yet, do it your way,
You say, you went to my high school
Then why can't I find you?

I have looked in every grade
For six years every way
And still I can't find you.

I have looked in basketball, football, and track
I have been looking in the cooking class with others making snacks
And still I can't find you.

I have looked in the ROTC
I have looked in gym class before it was called PE
And still I can't find you.

I have looked for teachers and their pets
I have looked at the dances with soldier cadets
And still I can't find you.

I have looked in the index and senior listings,
I have looked in the lunch room and kitchen settings
But still I can't find you.

I have looked in the prom photos
I have looked in the hallways and locker no-nos
And still I can't find you.

So, do you exist?
Or are you trying to make an impression?
Did you not graduate from high school?
And this is what you are trying not to mention?
For you see
I still can't find you.

Jack the Hammer Meets Betty Crocker

Incoming Carp E-mail: Somewhat attractive Fish with Bette Davis eyes. I am known for holding women hostage, wining them into a drunken stupor, playing Peeping Tom through glass windows, and then expecting them to spend a night with my musical snoring. Boat Launching and Docking 101 is required.

> *Miss Twye was soaping her breasts in the bath when she heard behind her a meaning laugh And to her amazement she discovered a wicked man in the bathroom cupboard.*
>
> *—Gavin Buchanan Ewart, "Miss Twye"*

Introduction: Big girls should understand the big ideas and the big plans of single men, especially if they are on leg seven of a marathon summer of fishing. I should have listened to Anne Lamott and the wisdom from her book *Plan B*. She believed in back-up plans, and I could have followed suit by writing helpful hints on sticky notes to be placed inside my bra for safekeeping. It is the best place for a reminder once things begin to go awry in the waters with Carp. But alas, with no paper, no pen, and no thoughts in my Plan A head, my bra is filled only with my breasts. With Jack the Hammer as leg seven, or 25.9 miles of my 26.6 mile race, I know in my heart I will have to take another break from fishing and give the last 0.7 mile to myself as a gift to insure sanity if I ever plan to graduate to middle school fishing.

The Novella: From a friend, I learned that Jack the Hammer was notorious for his ways with a hammer. He was skilled in carpentry, pipe

95

laying, landscaping, and anything else involving pounding. Putting Jack together with his hammer provided a completely different outcome, which will unfold in this experience under the guise of best intent. After a few phone calls, we planned a meeting the next day at Jack's house and to spend time on his boat in western Michigan at Lake Mackerela (which is not to be confused with Lake Macatawa). Lake Mackerela is anywhere in the world where events are pounded out with a Carp, if a gal feels unlucky enough to have snagged one. As we all know, Carp are not keepers, so we throw them back or feed them to the farm animals that are allergic to corn feed.

Both Jack and I entered this fishing scene on a high note. The phone conversation the night before went well. Jack had a nice voice and seemed friendly, and both of us loved boating, swimming, and Lake Mackerela. I made the error of making too much of his friendly voice and forgetting one of my Thou Shalt Nots with regard to Plan B—a possible escape plan—and did not take the time the night before to write one down on a sticky note and place it inside my bra. Victoria's Secret makes great gel bras with slits that are easy for hiding notes; they do not give the appearance of pointed bras reminiscent of the 1950s.

Jack greeted me at the door. I found him attractive in a buggy kind of way since he had big Bette Davis eyes, which are strange on a man. They were also yellow and marred with ribbons of red blood vessels. At one time, I am sure they were brilliant blue, but with time and life, there was only a hint of the youthful color.

Next, he walked me over to his pride and joy, his boat. To me, it was a huge wooden tugboat built circa the turn of the century. It was red in color, definitely needed a couple of coats of new paint, could not rival the SS *Minnow* nor find Gilligan and his island, and did not look like it could make it to Lake Mackerela, let alone motor on the waters. I am sure the Professor and Skipper would agree. Hopefully, it came equipped with oars, a blow horn, and flares to signal the Coast Guard. As a first line of defense, yelling "fire" was also a thought.

Jack promised we would be back before dark and that I could leave my car at this house. I was an idiot. There was no way we were going to make it to Lake Mackerela and back hauling the huge tugboat attached to his beater pickup truck. Bradley Cooper would agree, "That's not going to happen." Instead of making up a Plan B, I agreed and nodded my head like the bobble head on his dashboard. I felt even worse once we began the drive; the pickup only reached a maximum speed of thirty-five miles an hour.

During the drive to hell, which is where I was sure I was going, Jack stopped at a local Mackerels and Spirits Shop and told me to pick out anything my little heart desired. So we bought tuna steaks, deli salads, fresh grapes, fresh green beans, and plenty of *vino blanco* or white wine. The cash for the day was on him. I forgot my commandment with regard to money as a nonnegotiable with unknown Carp and sealed my fate with some kind of execution; on a big lake, water torture came to mind.

Jack may have been jacked up with a hammer but I was all jacked up with anxiety and no Xanax in my purse. I lost my will with my spine and arrived at Lake Macherela drug free and with no sticky notes. Oh well, what the hell. He launched the boat and it did float, so all seemed well. We headed out of the channel and into deeper waters. Jack then told me he would close the door of the cabin so I could change into my bathing suit. Below, I noticed a glass partition at the top of the door and saw Jack staring at me like a Peeping Tom. I should have yelled out, "No peeking or I will come out with a hammer and aim for between your eyes and what's down below," but I chose to ignore him. Just when I thought I should cease to be amazed at the antics of a Carp, this one raised the bar, thus increasing my lack of expectations with regard to the species.

Dressed in my bathing suit with "nowhere to run and nowhere to hide" (and Martha Reeves and the Vandellas ironically playing on the stereo), I climbed the three stairs, opened the door, and greeted Jack. He was now seated on the back boat seat with his arms outstretched, making a cupping motion with his hands. I knew all too well the cups were to hold my breasts. It seemed much too early to be at the fondling stage, and besides, I was not attracted to him, nor did I feel any chemistry. The biggest factor was lack of chemistry. I was sure Jack failed chemistry since he was interested in attaching his hands to my breasts, which is content related to anatomy. I don't mind mixing up the sciences but prefer someone who has knowledge and interest in sparking me before fondling.

After making wrong choices this day, I was stuck with making the best of the worst of it. The afternoon actually became a crap shoot of the fifty-fifties. The good fifty cents included the food, getting completely hammered on the wine (which compensated for the lack of Xanax), and jumping and swimming from the boat as a solo effort. Jack told me he liked to be *on* the water, not *in* the water. I found this absurd and should have introduced Jack to Woodcock, since the two of them choose recreation in which they do not participate. I guess some people feel they only have to show up and everything else will fall into place. The bad fifty-cent crap included an afternoon and evening of trying to outrun Jack and his cupped hands. Jack certainly was a breast man. I should have brought along a chicken. With no chicken in hand, the hands caught me a couple of times, tackled me a few more, did a few whatevers with his hammer, and then he passed out.

Best to say, I spent one of the worst nights of my life on a tugboat without Gilligan to my rescue. Jack's snoring was relentless. It was lucky for him (and sad for me) that the refrigerator didn't come with a package of frozen peas and carrots to shove up his nose. I could have then mailed him north to Peas and Carrots, and the two of them could spend the rest of their days sorting vegetables.

I love using the word "hammered," because it has such a nice ring to it. Well, I need to reevaluate my liking of this word and remember it is only to be used when referencing getting crazy drunk and falling asleep on my back in the front yard of my house with my best gal friend Maggie, in Cabo where everything is Cabo-licious, or with my dear friend Tony who used the word to describe me during a visit with *Sarah Plain and Tall* stupid. Any other "hammered" is not acceptable.

I'm changing Jack's last name from Hammer to Mallet. Actually, Jack the Mullet is even better since his curly hair resembles the so-called hair fashion do. Jack the Mullet can then keep company with Betty Crocker. Betty is known for working with a variety of cups in her hands.

At 7:00 a.m., I can bear no more. I wake Jack and tell him I have to go home since I am hosting a family reunion for the afternoon and needed to "pick up the cheeses." I love this line about cheeses, which comes from the movie *Burn After Reading* with John Malkovich, Tilda

Swinson, Brad Pitt, and George Clooney. Who else could pull off a line about cheeses other than the Coen brothers?

With his mullet strewn in every direction, his older blues half open, and his jaw slack, Jack tried to wake up but mostly looked dead. He told me I had to help him get the boat out of the water. What this meant was he stood at the launch with his beater pickup and guided me so I was able to drive the boat onto the trailer. This was truly scary. I can dock my small boat but this tugboat was going to be a challenge. I said nothing and prayed I was able to follow his command. The thought of Bette Davis eyes with a red pattern of blood vessels exploding due to my error in judgment with docking was not a motion picture I planned to see. I'll give these rights to the Coen brothers and Quentin Tarintino. Maybe they will want to burn it after reading.

Jack waved at me and motioned with his hands to move forward very slowly. Thoughts of peas and carrots have my hands frozen. His face showed he was losing patience and again he waved for me to move in his direction. I gently moved the throttle forward and hoped and prayed I did not drive the boat up onto the concrete parking lot or, worse yet, run him and his beater pickup truck over and flatten them like sand dollars. Secretly, this would not have been a bad outcome.

I surprised myself and did a wonderful job of driving the boat up onto the trailer. Jack did not even acknowledge my effort. I really didn't care. I just wanted to pick up the cheeses and be home and in bed. We drove back to his house in silence.

We arrived at Jack's house, and I got in my car without even saying good-bye. I made it home in time to sleep for one hour before I had a house full of people, and no one picked up the cheeses. Oh well, what the hell, Velveeta works just as well.

Epilogue: A few weeks later, I bumped into a friend of Jack's, who told me some Jack news. It seemed he got a silly notion he could appear as a regular on "Celebrity Apprentice" with Brett Michaels. Brett told him he already won the apprenticeship and is now working for Mr. Trump. Besides, Jack is not a celebrity and does not qualify to enter the boardroom.

Jack's response to Brett was, "I am one; I wrote a song and it is called 'If I Had a Hammer.'" Brett told him the song was released in the 1960s and to give up his hammer and find a different tool or, better yet, write a song entitled "If I Had a Mullet." They discussed possible lyrics and came up with a catchy first verse, "If I had a mullet, I'd wear it in the morning, I'd wear it in the evening, all over this land. I'd ring out to repeat offenders, red neckers, woodpeckers, and tailgaters all over this land." Jack was last seen as a rising star on You Tube singing songs with Mullets Incorporated.

> *The Mullet's sleeping position is known as a Ponytail.*
> *Originally it was thought the Ponytail was a subspecies*
> *of Mullets, but it is now known that the Mullet will*
> *reduce its width and be allowed to be tied back.*
>
> —*Author Unknown*

Time Out: It is now the end of my marathon summer of fishing with Carp, and once again it is time for me to take a break. Postponing fishing until after the first of the year will give me time to do the important things like taking care of my mental and emotional health, throwing out all the mayonnaise from my fridge, buying extra hammers to round out the dents in my head, and stock up on toilet paper. I need more than a summer vacation before I enter middle school and adolescent fishing.

Part III
Middle School: Adolescent Fishing

I think that is a universal adolescent feeling, trying
to find your place. The adolescent who is perfectly
adjusted to his environment, I've yet to meet.

—*Roger Bannister*

Asics

Incoming Carp E-mail: Successful businessman with homes in a few places. My life is extremely busy in a good way since I am always running off to a new adventure. I am interested in finding a wife and mother to my six children, who are all under the age of twelve.

> *I always loved running ... it was something you could do by yourself, and under your own power. You could go in any direction, fast or slow as you wanted, fighting the wind if you felt like it, seeking out new sights just on the strength of your feet and the courage of your lungs.*
>
> —*Jesse Owens*

Introduction: After thirty-two years of pounding the pavement and gravel with my love of distance running, I am still in love with my Asics. They are one of my favorite running shoes due to the wide toe-box. With more than half of my life on the road, my feet have taken on a life of their own. Both feet now come equipped with huge bunions and toenails that forgot how to grow. My doctor once said to me I had more miles on my legs than his car. This made me smile proudly. On the belly side of the fish, a little girl told my daughter-in-law Robin that my feet freaked her out. Robin said, "Her feet are fine. That's what they look like after a lifetime of running." Her reply: "They still freak me out."

The Novella: From the outset, I was drawn to this Fish, who I will refer to as Asics, for all the right reasons. His photo and biography offered possibilities since the both of us came equipped with adventurous spirits and also had lost a spouse. I really do put stock in spouses with deceased partners as possible companions, since their past was changed due to circumstances completely out of their control. This does not happen in divorce, but in death; a partner does not usually choose to die. These are just a few my reflective thoughts with regard to the death of my husband. I would certainly understand if you chose to disagree or thought differently.

Even though the initial fishing seemed the most likely to support both the widow and widower, like any relationship, it does pose challenges. Examples include the length of the illness, how long the surviving spouse was a caregiver, whether the death was due to a sudden accident, the relationship prior to the death, and the length of grief time.

Asics was ten years younger than me. From experience, I have learned some men are without ego and age is not an issue, so I thought this may be the case. I did notice several of his photos were with a number of family members, and his biography mentioned that he had six children. He looked extremely happy so I said yes.

We decided to meet for lunch, even though I was second-guessing myself. I had just returned from a vacation in Mexico, with browner than brown sugar skin, but also dealing with some sort of illness associated with change in climate and flying in multiple planes with multiple people and multiple germs. None of this was new news to me. Regardless, I decided to meet Asics, since I was all dressed up to see Lady Gaga, via a webcast, reciting the lyrics to "Telephone" in iambic pentameter. I was curious which lyrics would fit the ten syllable pattern. Even Shakespeare had a difficult time convincing the Poet Laureate Scratching Heads Society that "to be or not to be, that is the question" was ten syllables since "question" has two syllables, making the line eleven. So if Shakespeare can get away with it, I am sure Lady Gaga will be able to convince the groupies with user names and pin numbers that "stop calling, stop calling, I don't want to talk anymore" fits the pattern. After studying lyrics of my favorites, I found that Kid Rock is the king of iambic pentameter since "3 sheets 2 the winds is the state I'm in" is exactly ten syllables.

With sniffles coming from my nose, sweat coming out of the hair on top of my head and back of my neck, and feeling like a candidate for Encased and Embalmed Respiratory Burials, I met Asics at a quaint eatery located in a professional building called Vegetables and Spirits. I knew him immediately because I saw the nice crinkles at the corners of his blue eyes, athletic build, and clothing with Eastbay logo; he looked exactly like his online photo. From the history with Mayo, I am sure you understand this is of the utmost importance with regard to appearances.

We made some small talk and ordered our grilled vegetables; the closest I can get to spirits is tea. What a crazy name for an establishment, along with a crazy menu and beverage selection. This is the only time where I will actually use the word "beverage," since it is such a nonword to describe a liquid much like a nonword to describe this eatery. I guess most people order wine with vegetables. It is hard to fathom getting all liquored up over a plate of grilled eggplant.

Chatter now turned to the sixty-four-million-dollar questions, including widowhood and children, with my grown sons as self-sufficient and Asics with more than a Two Live Crew to chase. I was in the listening mode but was unable to process the math since critical thinking does not come with respiratory infections and burial rites. Thus, I had no idea that time with Asics will not be spent running down the road as a twosome, which I do not do anyway.

Lunch was more than over, like a dead blue gill bitten in half by a musky, and we parted, with Asics asking me to dinner on Saturday. I was *Sarah Plain and Tall* stupid and told him to give me a call at an appropriate time. Once in my car and on my way to becoming cultured with the likes of Lady Gaga, who should take direction from Kid Rock with regard to iambic pentameter, my nose seemed to dry up and the sweat was gone. My thoughts in my little head contributed this to a diet of vegetables and spirits. Lady Gaga did not disappoint me, and I was now versed with her musical connection to Shakespeare. I wondered if he was a long-distance relative, since they both sport huge collars to frame their necks as fashion statements.

Saturday afternoon arrived, and all of a sudden I had a massive headache. I felt like I just ran into a Mack truck and there was no highway in sight. The Mack truck was my lunch date with Asics. Quickly, I did a play it backwards and remembered a lot of bumps in the road, even with a good pair of running shoes. Asics was ten years younger than me (bump), he was a widower (bump, bump), he has six kids under the age of twelve (bump, bump, bump), and he spends Saturdays going to soccer, dance, karate, photography, and Science Olympiad (bump, bump, bump, bump). I fell over a stone and crashed. I needed a huge Band-Aid, and it had to be the kind made of durable fabric and not latex with Incredible Hulk pictures.

Yes, Asics is a nice guy, has crinkles at the corners of his blue eyes, loves vegetables and spirits, but has kids not related to the species known as goat. Aged over fifty, I am in the panther stage of my life, and I am pretty sure panthers are a species not equipped to mingle with goats. In fact, I am pretty sure in the jungles of Africa, panthers eat goats. I am not about eating someone else's kids, but I am pretty sure you get the picture. Panthers only come equipped with the ability to nurture grandkids.

Saturday evening approached, and Asics and Willie Nelson are probably home from the road again after acquiring miles and miles of soccer, dance, karate, photography, and Science Olympiad bumps. Yes, the phone rang with Asics telling me about his day; then he asked if seven o'clock was a good time for dinner. Instead of going off the deep end of the pool and telling him I failed the time trials for the Boston Marathon, I told him the truth. Sincerely, I said no date, no dinner, not in your house as a guest with six children, no way. It was not fair to either one of us, especially the children.

There was dead, awkward silence on the other end. Asics said he was sorry about the way I felt and wished things could have been different. I said I wished so too, but I was not ready to run into his house full of children. Out of respect for his entire family, I was not the person he should be dating. I know only too well how my grown sons would react to this situation with another possible male figure in the house other than their father, and they are adults. Second-guessing what was going on in the minds of little ones whose mother had died was analysis for Asics. I thanked him for his time and said good-bye.

Epilogue: In the end, it was what it was. I was grateful I was not of the desperate species and did not make the choice to continue fishing, running, and trying to keep up with Asics' family life. I did not consider him a Carp. He had the best interest with regard to his children, and I am confident there is someone who will one day embrace and love his family. Also, I honor his spirit and love of vegetables.

I feel confident knowing I have graduated to middle school and did not make a foolhardy decision, possibly adding jeopardy to a family who has experienced the pain of losing a lover and mother. This statement is not profound but emotional common sense.

Though I am not naturally honest, I am sometimes by chance.
—William Shakespeare

I'm Dull

Telephone rings, Lady Gaga melody sings.
Man on the other end
Wants to know if I am who I am.

I say yes, who are you?
I think I may be a possible
Mate for you.

Do you have time to talk?
Yes, I do, tell me a bit about you.
Hour and half later it all boils down
To one last sentence with his summation as resound.

I am dull, most people find,
So you will have to get to know me with time.
Time, how much time,
How much time before I do not see you as dull?

After six to eight dates is fair
It gives me plenty of time to share
And for you to see that it is fine to be dull
I have other things that you will find endearing.

I love to read and just sit on the porch
I walk by myself and can be absorbed with nothing for hours
You don't need me.
You need a dog.
Name him Dull.

Time and Mathematics

Incoming Carp E-mail: I am a widower trying to move forward and find a companion. The time with my loss has been a little over a year. I feel confident I am a perfect match as a fisher of women and not a Carp in any way, shape, or form. Please fish with me.

> *Time is free, but it's priceless. You can't own it, but you can use it. You can't keep it, but you can spend it. Once you've lost it, you can never get it back.*
>
> —*Harvey MacKay*

Preface: After Asics, I did take a time-out, in fact about five months of time, but still considered this period of time as middle school dating. One Fish does not determine a final grade, nor do all widowers come with small children. So I was back to the fishing pond and open to another, whatever the line reeled in. This Fish I will call Time.

Introduction: Time was someone I knew in passing but not really personally. We happened to frequent the same places, like the Lettuce Be Your Friend grocery store and the Put Your Stuff in Here local bank. I always wondered why I could not meet a decent man in the grocery store, since I spent so much time there. After this event, I will check out Home Depot. I have more use for paintbrushes than a head of lettuce.

The Novella: One winter day, I found myself in the Lettuce Be Your Friend grocery store checkout line; Time was waiting in front of me.

We exchanged hellos and made idle chitchat about nothing. I did not think too much of our grocery store meeting.

In the parking lot, I began to unload my groceries into the trunk of my car. Time was parked right behind me and honked his horn. I waved and then thought, how strange. If my husband were alive, he had better not be honking at (in addition to talking to) other women. I had thought Time was still married, but then I learned from a follow-up phone call to a friend that his wife had died. So armed with this information, I got over the weirdness of the situation at the grocery store and decided to make an advance.

At first, I was a little apprehensive with the thought of calling Time, but in the end, it became a phone call to do and another one of my "Oh well, what the hell" kind of decisions. He did not answer the phone, so I left a message, telling him it was nice to see him at Lettuce Be Your Friend and inviting him to meet at a time of his choosing. He never returned my phone call. I interpreted this as not being ready for another woman. This conclusion made the most sense since it took me over two years before I could actually entertain the thought, let alone be with another man.

A few months passed, and once again, I bumped into Time, this time at the Put Your Stuff in Here local bank. We were at separate drive-up windows, so I honked my horn. He smiled and rolled down his window. I mentioned I had called a few months ago and asked if he received my message. He said no. I thought that was strange but let it go. I told him I would call when I got home. I am a person of honor, so I called, left a message, and waited. Waiting for time to pass is something I do not do well, even though it involves math.

I measured the time, and it was fifteen minutes before Time returned my phone call. He apologized for not returning the first call but it really was not his fault. His response was that the message may have been erased due to a power outage. I thought about what a crock the story was, but it is not a big crock. It is more of an irritation that could fit into a fondue pot. The irritation became a hash mark on the mental math chart known as my forehead. It is flat like a piece of paper.

The phone conversation continued with Time asking me if I would like to come over to his house to chat and have a beverage. I had heard the idiot word beverage before from Bucky the Tooth and added another hash mark to my forehead, which dissolved any concentration with regard to our conversation. I found my mind downshifting into a blurry state due to visually focusing on trying to figure out the circumference of Time's bald head. I should have said no at that point, but with no point, I decided to say yes.

I thanked him for offering his house and considered this a better option, since I don't plan on bringing any more Carp to my house. I do not want to give the neighbors anything to think or stink about, so keeping the fumes at his house was a good choice. Besides, I did know him casually and did not think he was of the dangerous species who would answer the door with a fillet knife, six-prong lure, or a fish net. So with a few hash marks on my forehead, we decided to meet at six o'clock the next evening. My hopes were the hash marks did not require more space than my forehead could accommodate.

Next evening came, and I was dressed in three pieces of clothing and flip-flops. The three pieces of clothing were nothing unusual for summer and consisted of a smock bra top, capris, and my underwear. I love summer, and the idea of less is more. I love online shopping even more.

The drive to Time's house took no time at all. His house was of the less-is-more distance, and this was good math with gas mileage for Beulah, my wonderful automobile. Time greeted me at the door with a nice smile. I would have liked to use the word "warm" to describe his smile, but that conjures too much emotion, and I am not sure he is a fella who is hot, damn hot.

We sat on opposite ends of the couch, and he asked if I would like a beverage. There it was again, the "beverage" word. The word made me cringe like fingernails drawn on a chalkboard. If I could swear in math terms, I would be shouting expletives like he never heard before: calculus, binominals, trapezoid, functions, altitude, cylinder, pi circumference, and zero. Instead, I tell him no, I am fine, and make another hash mark on my forehead for the word "beverage." I wondered if I would ever be able to block the word "beverage" and Bucky the Tooth from my mind. I needed to figure out how to get past these images. Another time and another place may bring resolution. It certainly won't be this time with Time.

We spent the next three hours in discussion, or rather he asked about the loss of my spouse and I poured out my heart like an emotional slut. The time since my loss had been longer than Time's, and he seemed genuinely interested. So the agenda became a series of questions, a much longer series of bringing things from the past to the present, and even much longer time of emotional duress to the point where I was sadly exhausted. There was no way I was going to break down and cry in front of him. Instead, I was thinking of peeing.

I questioned how much longer this conversation was going to last. I had sat for three hours and I definitely had to pee. It was one thing to cry in front of someone but it was totally another thing to pee. Taking a pee and running the water at the same time was something I could not do in his house. Peeing with a total stranger was much easier. I knew this for a fact since I peed in front of lots of strange men in European restrooms. Most of the time, I did not have Euros and chose to pee at the common urinal. But peeing, standing at the same time, running water, and trying to figure out the circumference of Time's bald head were all out of the question. His big, bald head was really causing emotional duress, and my thinking was that older men are regressing to the birth state in which the head is the biggest part exiting the vaginal chute. Men's big heads resemble mice trying to get into the house through a light socket without a cover (I know this since the entry way for the socket is where most mice turds are found).

After three hours, and more math in my head, I had had it. The conversation was draining, and I felt like I had been sucked dry; my peeing thoughts disappeared for a moment. Where did the urine go? It had been here for the past three hours. Maybe it evaporated through my skin, much like garlic. I'd have to remember to add a sticky note in my bra telling me to always wear a catheter under my smock bra top. Peeing and talking while sitting on the sofa is something I can do at the same time. This does not involve standing, and I need my knees for running.

I was drained and still staring at Time's head and trying to guesstimate the circumference; he used this opportune time to tell me he was seeing someone else. Well, circle up those horses and find Ward Bond and his wagon train, we are now back to the pattern stage of math, which is also known as number sense, which I do not have.

Why in the hell didn't he tell me this from the outset? Why did he put me through so much misery for the past three hours? I felt like one of Bob Seger's silver bullets had pierced my heart. This was just plain cruel. I sat in silence for a moment, gained my composure, said absolutely nothing, and then got up to leave. I was mentally hash-marked out. My forehead was visibly bleeding, and I didn't bring any fabric Band-Aids without pictures of the Incredible Hulk.

Before I was able to make a slow getaway, Time stopped me at my car door and said he would like to show me something. Instead of saying I didn't have time, I just remembered I have to pee, I left my catheter at home, or my smock bra top is on backwards, I once again played the part of *Sarah Plain and Tall* stupid and said all right. He led me like one of the horses not chosen to be a part of the wagon train to his pole barn. In the barn, he stored his pride and joy, a 1969 silver Eldorado. It was beautiful and added more hash marks to my forehead. Why in the hell didn't he show me this when I was trying to keep my legs together? I wished I were a dog and could just lift my leg and pee on his shiny chrome hub cap and had enough left over to pee on his shoe.

I was in pain and exhausted, but Time was not finished with my time. The next words out of his mouth added enough hash marks for a beheading. He told me the next time he saw me, we would be riding in this car together (the one with the chrome dripping with pee that has the same DNA as the stain on his shoe). What in the hell is that supposed to mean? You are seeing someone else! I am not a gal who swears regularly, but at this point, I am certain Elizabeth Banks and prudence would agree it is more than time to drop the F-bomb.

The drive home only had me thinking of peeing. My bladder was overextended, my heart held a silver bullet, and I felt like I was suffering from emotional slutism and seriously thinking of checking into the Institute of the Mathematically Insane. Once admitted, two goals had to be accomplished before I could return home: a skin grafting to my forehead to smooth over the mental math hash marks and therapy to help me stop trying to figure out the circumference of Time's bald head. Actually, I would love to measure his head and then do a comparison check with heads of lettuce, cauliflower, and cabbage at Lettuce Be Your Friend. I wonder if there is room in the produce aisle for a head of Time.

Epilogue: A year later, I spotted Time, of course, at the local Lettuce Be Your Friend. He was looking at labels on the wrappers of loaves of bread, and I decided to skirt down the aisle with wine and pick up five bottles of Riesling (for me) and a box of white wine (to pass off as good wine for any incoming Carp). Then I bolted through the rest of the aisles throwing in (by guess or by gosh, I better have it today, otherwise it is a week away) the rest of what I needed. I even managed to throw in a white dotted Swiss skirt with lace trim (which I had to take back since it was too big and made me look like I was playing dress-up for Betty Crocker's homecoming party). Anyway, I made it to the *Bruce Almighty* aisle and was about to check out (in more ways than one). I did not see Time, so I began to unload my cart at warp speed. Too bad Oxy and his band of silent women weren't with me. With his lightning-speed tongue, we would have already been out the door and down the road.

Magically, because I have no better transition word to use at this time, Time strolled down the aisle and ended up two rows down from my check-out lane. Oh nuts to the guy with no nuts or balls and his choice of check-out lanes. I didn't even look at him, paid the cashier, and pushed the full cart (mostly full of liquids) out the door and to my car. Popping open the trunk, I tossed everything inside and thought I had almost made my awful get-away. But nuts to nuts (and most of the time they are peanuts) struts the biggest walnut of all, right down the same parking aisle as me.

Time was about twenty feet from me and gave me a big smile. I couldn't tell if it was from nerves or genuineness. I banked it was on nerves since he was such a big Focker. Again, I was looking at his head and trying to guess the circumference. My guesstimate is about thirty-five inches, add or subtract an inch. I am pretty good at ballparking numbers, and I guesstimate his waist at forty inches, so his head must be at least thirty-five inches. I think that makes good sense and reasoning using intellectual risk as a factor.

Long story short, Time tried to make small talk, since that was the only talk he was capable of; he asked me mindless questions about blah, blah, blah. I wasn't even listening. For all I knew, he may have split with Ray Parker and was no longer in love with the other woman and was now interested in me. Now that was a scary thought. Anyway, what the hay, I drove off into the bright sun, stopped and petted my favorite dog that does not belong to me, gave him his Thursday free chew bone, opened the doors to my house, and let the cats out. Life is good with cats. They always greet me with a big yawn saying, "Thank you for not bringing home a Focker." I wouldn't mind if they dropped the F-bomb since they are prudent with its use.

A broken heart is what makes life so wonderful five years later,
when you see the guy in an elevator and he is fat and smoking
a cigar and saying 'long time no see.' If he hadn't broken
your heart, you couldn't have that glorious feeling of relief!

—*Phyllis Battell*

Cindy Lucy

The New Math with New Men

Grade school years brought on many fears,
one would wonder through the years.
How am I going to learn basic math?
It is really quiet simple, just rely on basic facts.
Basic facts are 1+1 = 2 and 2 + 2 = 4,
Or even 6 + 4 = 10.

Golden years bring a new school of facts.
One of these is new math at an exponential rate.
Long ago, I learned that 6 + 4 = 10 was correct,
but how does 6 + 4 = 0 today relate?
Have I lost my mind in the oodles of facts?
Can I no longer do simple math as a matter of fact?
Did I lose my car in the parking lot at Sears?
No, no, no, it is the fact of new math, my dears,
6 + 4 = 0.

New math comes to us in the golden years
when the history of our lives has added more than
numbers to our years.
We marry and we procreate, and have offspring at an exponential rate,
Multiple wives and multiple children skew our fate.
6 + 4 = 0

When once upon a time 4 + 6 = 10,
It is now apparent that 4 + 6 = 0 instead of ten.
Uno mas no mas is his deal,
He is stuck with his basic math fact that is his real.
4 + 6 = 0

For a smarter woman in her golden years,
understands basic math facts and has learned
to hold true to elementary days when 6 + 4 = 10.

Golden-years fella is stuck with his fate,
which can't be undone at any rate.
It is much too late for him to undo,
4 + 6 = 0

Part IV
High School Fishing

In high school you can think you're in love, but I believe you have to know yourself completely before you can truly fall in love and be loved back by someone else.

—*Author Unknown*

Interesting

New mail, new male, how fun
From a forty-four-year-old bachelor on the run
Who says he only dates older women, no drama, more fun,
From a forty-four-year-old bachelor on the run.
Interesting.

New mail, new male, how fun
From the forty-four-year-old bachelor with no drama, more fun
No wife and no babies for thee
Older women are out of procreating activity
From a forty-four-year-old bachelor on the run.
Interesting.

New mail, new male, how fun
From the forty-four-year-old bachelor looking to the sun
Visions of next words he chooses unthinkingly
What are your measurements?
And I stare at the computer incomprehensibly
From a forty-four-year-old bachelor on the run.
Not interesting.

New mail, old male, not fun
Standing soaking wet at five foot three
and light on the pounds at one hundred twelve plus three
The rest of the measurements pretty much fit
Even my deceased husband never once inquired a bit
No mail, no male, no fun
From the forty-four-year-old bachelor who will continue on the run.
Blocked.

Aqua Boy

Incoming Carp E-mail: I am a confirmed bachelor, have a good service record, and give scuba diving lessons at vacation resorts. I am looking for a somewhat older woman. I have heard they are more skilled in the art of love making and not as demanding.

> *Loving an old bachelor is always a no-win situation, and*
> *you come to terms with that early on, or you go away.*
>
> —*Jean Harris*

Introduction: Once upon a time, my gal friend Patti Cakes asked me to take a vacation to Maui. She had won timeshare points at a church gambling event as the runner-up. The first place winner chose the prize of two acres of property in Fairbanks, Alaska, with permafrost located only four feet below the surface. What this means is when the winner is building a new condo in the land of ice and snow, he will hit ice after only digging down four feet. In order to install a septic and well system, he'll have to put fire in the hole, melting the ice, and then dig the remains with a backhoe. This process continues until the hole is deep enough to sink piping for indoor plumbing. Patti got lucky and won the better prize.

The Novella: When Patti and I had visited Kauai, we were not happy with the weather, since Kauai is the wettest place on the earth. With her timeshare winnings, we decided to do a second Hawaiian vacation but this time to Maui. Patti told me she referenced the Book of Revelations according to the Book of Cakes, which stated that the weather in Maui is perfect every day and does not have chickens running around or cockfights in the local Wal-Mart parking lot. I don't think Maui even has a Wal-Mart and do not remember any pictures of Jennifer Anniston or Jennifer Love-Hewitt on the cover of *The Star* chasing cocks away from their car as they try to load deals purchased from the center aisle. So no chickens, no cocks, and good weather get the all-is-well vote from me.

Patti told me our friend Tag-a-Long would be joining us. This was bad news to me. I asked her why in the heck she decided to invite her. I can only take about ten minutes of her whining (which is not associated with wining), her tight-as-a-drum attitude with regard to money, her feigned helplessness, and her obsession with lipstick. I swear the woman has a separate carry-on just to accommodate all the colors somewhere over the rainbow. I am sure she even has a color that matches Dorothy's shoes. Patti told me that Tag-a-Long twisted her arm behind her back, so she had to invite her. Tag-a-Long also dropped the F-bomb instead of calling Patti a Focker.

The next day, we three as company arrived in Maui. We quickly unpacked our bags and headed down to the pool. All I could think about was that I was in Maui—a dream come true, and I had never had this dream before. Beside the pool were dozens of lounge chairs, so we found three together, lathered up our bodies with oil, and decided to do our jet-lag day in the sun. One thing was missing: a Bloody Mary, the breakfast of chumpions. With no Cheerios, a Bloody Mary was my vacation favorite. I knew Tag-a-Long was going to ask me to make the trip to the bar, so I offered instead, to keep her from blowing up and twisting my arm behind my back and calling me a Focker. I didn't mind having my arm twisted behind my back, but being called a Focker in public was over the limit.

At the bar, the pool boy, who I will call Aqua Boy, walked over to me and began some idle chitchat. He told me he was the scuba instructor and had been so for the past eight years. His past work in the navy allowed him to give scuba lessons and then spend the rest of his day swimming through trenches with vacationers. All of this was good information for the offering, but I was completely puzzled why he picked me as the shareholder. With my peripheral vision, I scanned the area to see if I could find a Professor Plum clue as to why Aqua Boy singled me out from all the other women at the resort. It appeared I was one of the few gals who was under sixty years of age, single, and came equipped with guns and a six-pack. Also, I was wearing a red honky-tonk bikini, so I came to the conclusion I attracted a Peter on my first day in Heaven.

Aqua Boy Peter asked me out to dinner for the evening, and I said yes. I was hoping he would take me to a place with pearly gates. If the gates were made out of wrought-iron, I could always call Tag-a-Long to help me escape, since her surefire mouth of Fockers could cut through anything made of steel and iron. I could take care of the pearls all by myself.

At seven o'clock, Aqua Boy picked me up at the front entrance in a car he must have bought from Lazy Dukes. It was a faded blue Catalina with a two-by-four as the back bumper. I was in shock since I thought all old cars died in Mexico. My favorite Mexican vendor in Puerto Vallarta told me the reason that all old cars find their way to Mexico is because it is their slice of Heaven after spending a lifetime in miserable weather in the states. Aqua Boy saw the full orchestra of dismay on my face and told me his truck was being repaired and this vehicle was the only loaner. I asked him if any bikes were available. Riding to the restaurant in tandem seemed more romantic than riding down Maui Boulevard in the car that Lazy built.

Riding to the restaurant, I saw no one looking, no one cared, and there weren't any stares. Aqua Boy dropped me off at the front door and said he would meet me once he parked the so-called love mobile. If he thought he was doing anything else with me besides eating, he was going to have to wine and dine me and make sure he gets his regular vehicle back.

Things turned for the better once we had time to dine and chat. I really liked Aqua Boy. He made me feel so young, just like a teenage girl without an appetite. I felt like I had a permanent smile on my face, and looking into his eyes faded the thought of riding back to the resort in the Catalina that belonged in a Mexican heaven. Maybe someone would steal it while we were eating and we could take a cab back.

Aqua Boy was a complete gentleman. I didn't even mind the return ride to the resort. He dropped me off at the side entrance, since the resort was his place of employment. I felt like the high school girl who was coming home late and didn't want to wake up her parents. I liked this little naughty escapade of sneaking around in the dark. It reminded me of 1974 and Robert Palmer singing, "Sneakin Sally through the alley trying to keep her out of sight when out pops the wife." To make it even a little naughtier, instead of a good-night kiss, Aqua Boy gave me a full boob squeeze and asked if he could see me again tomorrow. He suggested a visit to his house and grounds and then a scuba lesson and swimming in the trenches. Nothing would keep me away from spotting a moray eel, and I told him to pick me up at one o'clock.

The next day, Aqua Boy arrived on time in his bright red Dodge Ram pickup truck. He looked so cute and boyish with his red hair and freckles; the night before, he lied and said he was forty-two when I told him I was fifty-eight. I called him a liar and said he did not look a day over thirty-five. He lied and told me he thought I was forty-three. What a charmer. Friendly liars are fine with me. I liked Aqua Boy.

We drove up to an area where housing was at a premium; his little abode was sandwiched in like peanut butter and jelly of smaller places, offering balance to the community. Upon entering, I saw it was definitely a bachelor pad with all the most important assets: a bed, bathroom, and gym equipment. There was no other furniture. Aqua Boy wasted no time and pressed me against the wall, giving me a big hard kiss and not with the skill set taught in junior high with regard to only smooching and necking with no petting allowed. He kissed with his teeth! I was in shock. Had no one before this told him this is not kissing and is painful. I can't even figure out how anyone managed kissing with their teeth since the lips come first and are on the outside of the mouth. I had heard of rough sex but rough kissing had not happened to me since high school, where some guys did not know any better. Two lips on my two lips is called kissing, sticking your tongue in the well is called French kissing, and you only use your teeth when chewing a piece of steak or tobacco.

I said none of this to Aqua Boy and just pulled away, which was fine with him since the next thing that happened was we were both flat on the bed (with me on my flatter side). He turned my flatter side over to expose my backside and began to spank me, and I didn't even do anything wrong. I wondered if Judas Priest, from my pay-it-forward mind, and the rest of the Ukrainians were watching from the closet.

Aqua Boy was a Focker. Well, this was about enough. First, he bit my face off like Hannibal Lecter, and then spanked me as if he was friends with Judas Priest. I flipped over on my front side and asked him what all this biting and spanking was about. He said, "I'm just trying to find out what you like."

I said to him, "Did it ever cross your mind to just ask me? Me is telling you just regular stuff happens on the first date, even though it is technically our second date. No biting, spanking, whips, chains, handcuffs, or ceiling swings, and nothing that has to do with my suppository side is allowed."

After my Focker blow-up, everything went very smoothly and rhythmically. The next few minutes were just minutes, or it might have been closer to ten, of what Aqua Boy can actually do that is exactly right, and then out of my mouth came, "Is it time to go scuba diving?" It was soon enough to ask this since I do need my mouth to insert an air tube.

Scuba diving was out of the question since I have asthma. I wished he had told me this earlier, but now I understood the lesson was the carrot dangling in front of the pony. Instead, he suggested a two-mile walk on the grounds in the ninety-degree temperature. As a long-distance runner, this was not a problem, but Aqua Boy was definitely hot and bothered, and this had nothing to do with our chemistry. He had to stop a few times just to catch his breath. I looked at him and could not believe he was a boy and acting like an old man.

We returned to his house, he drove me back to the resort, and I was in time for happy hour (the price of drinks was two for the price of one).

The next day, Aqua Boy showed up at the pool, and I greeted him with a smile and a hello. I had no intentions of continuing the week as it started but still wanted to be on friendly terms. He looked at me, and I could see he was in serious pain. He told me he had thrown his back out and could not get meds until after his poolside shift, which was the end of the day. In the meantime, life went on, and vacationers wanted their scuba time. I actually felt sorry for him, even though he did bite off my mouth and spank me for no reason. Actually, I was over all the biting and spanking; no big deal.

Back at the pool, Patti told me her revelations according to the Book of Cakes. I was the root of Aqua Boy's maladies. He had no idea what he was getting himself into by befriending an older, younger gal who whacked out his back. I was worth a broken back and should be flattered. I was torn because I did know I was the reason he could barely walk but found it amusing, since most of the time this usually happened to women, and the hardly walking had nothing to do with our backs but it was from being on our backs. Aqua Boy ignored me for the rest of the week, and that was fine. Partying during happy hour and kissing other guys for fun was more fun.

It was the end of the week, and as Joe Walsh says, "Life's been good to me so far." Patti Cakes, Tag-a-Long, and I did not have any drama since the drama was on my channel of soap operas. If I could do this week over again, I would do it all the same way. How often can I say to someone, "Yes, I met a nice young fella with red hair and a red pickup truck, and I broke his back after he bit off my face. I am better off than Lady Gaga, who had a fella who 'ate her heart and then ate her brain.'" At least, I was left with vital organs intact.

I could only laugh and smile; something that should have happened to me in my twenties happened to me in my fifties. Maybe this was why they referred to this time of life as the golden years. It was actually golden (or priceless) to share some time with someone and actually walk away with my two lips intact and know that bowed legs only last for a maximum of two days.

Epilogue: Aqua Boy's back got better and he met another gal who also liked to be on her backside flipped around to her front side. He gave her a great big teeth-biting kiss, and she smacked him across the face and told him to buy a muzzle or better yet to take Kissing 101 at the nearest community college. After registering for the course and speaking to the instructor, Aqua Boy discovered the course work was to no avail and he should seek medical treatment. He did and was diagnosed with Oxygen Hose syndrome. It seemed after years of wearing an oxygen hose and face mask, his mouth had become distorted to the point where normal kissing was compromised and full frontal teeth mashing was the only option. The recommendation was a visit to Humptulips, Washington, which is known for its technological triumphs with regard to mouth abnormalities. A special kind of tulip is grown, and in its live form, attaches to the lips and heals the distortion. This healing takes two years, during which Aqua Boy must be quarantined to the grounds. In two years, I hope I meet Aqua Boy. I have faith in tulips.

> *The kiss originated when the first male reptile*
> *licked the first female reptile, implying in a subtle,*
> *complimentary way that she was as succulent as the*
> *small reptile he had for dinner the night before.*
>
> —*Author Unknown*

Mind Your Own Business

Catholic school taught me many things
Of this I do sing
Sister Mary Jane said
Mind Your Own Business
And life will bring you happiness.

Mind your own business
Has more than a ring
It is a lesson in life for single things.

When I mind other business
I never find what may matter most
It ends up being a fleeting glimpse
Of what I just lost I boast.

Minding my own business
I tell single gals
For when minding your own business
Is where the fish falls.

It may be in the grocery store or
At a crossing section or in the mall
But minding your own business
Can be a surprise to all.

For when looking for business
In finding other guys
Life is a mystery of
Where they are
Which is nowhere

But minding your own business
Wherever it may be
And a guy may just be waiting for thee.

Cindy Lucy

But minding your own business brings
Unsuspecting pleasure
And a smile to each
One may be in the liquor aisle
And one may be in the produce giving a squeeze
But minding your own business
Usually brings a fella as handsome as you please.

Oral Hygiene

Incoming Carp E-mail: I am a confirmed bachelor in my late forties and am interested in taking care of all my hygiene needs, more specifically oral. I enjoy frequent phone calls and am versed in fabricating stories to fit spontaneous moments.

A bachelor never quite gets over the idea that he
is a thing of beauty and a boy forever.
Marrying an old bachelor is like buying second-hand furniture.

—*Helen Rowland*

Introduction: As I look for the so-called "Big One," I have finally learned that trying to begin a relationship with a confirmed bachelor is a no-win situation for either of us. It may work for others, but it has not worked for me. I do know of one successful couple, but both are confirmed in that one is a bachelor and the other is a bachelorette.

The Novella: To date, I have met a few confirmed bachelors: Peas and Carrots, Aqua Boy, and the other one was Baby. I never really met Baby, but we did e-mail several times, and he still posts his endearing baby photo as a hook with bait. Anyway, once in a while I still hear from Baby, and I think he will always stay a Baby. Helen Rowland confirms my thoughts.

With this in mind, I received an e-mail from another confirmed bachelor. Before I responded, I decided to take my daily six-mile run and stopped to get advice from the Dolly Lama, who is a real-life lama residing at a nearby bed and breakfast. She provided a litany of wise questions; she seemed eager for gossip. Her questions included "Was his decision by choice? Does he have mother issues? Is he afraid of commitment? Is he dating-shy? Is he lazy or selfish?" After this litany, my only thought was he probably flunked chemistry and did not take Relationship Building 101 at Attracting the Other Sex Community College; therefore, he had no prerequisite training. I thanked Dolly and finished my run with no thoughts left in my head (thus, the reason I continue to run).

My return home finds another e-mail from Trunk, not his name but since he was so rooted in singlehood, I decided this would be a good name for a bachelor. Our time together was short, not sweet, and mostly just pure nonsense. Trunk told me he had a busy weekend with friends and asked if I would be interested in meeting him at a party. This seemed a little scary, since not only did I not know him, I would not know the others, and for all I know, they may be into bondage and heroin. Drugs are one thing, but thoughts of intimate sex on a first date with Bradley Cooper prompts his reminder, "that's not going to happen." I ask him what kind of party and where; it's on the other side of town with people my age, so it will probably be just a bunch of old bearded stoners. I told him this I could do and would meet him a little later in the evening. By then, the stoners will be stoned and having munchies and I can just slip in like the pocket knife I plan to carry in my pants' pocket.

Arriving at the party, I saw there was no need for my pocket knife. The people were as old as me and most of them were just getting off from having a beer and talking about Medicaid and retirement. The hottest topic was when to begin receiving Social Security benefits. I have learned to never discuss religion, politics, and finances, so I just smiled and was glad to at least eliminate drugs from this scene.

Even though no one really knew me, I felt like everyone did. I chatted with Trunk's friend, Lief, who told me this particular party was great in that more people showed up than usual. Maybe it was the nice weather, people did not have prior obligations, or after years of friendships, it was getting easier to make the commitment. Regardless, it seemed like the right factors coming together at the right time, in the right place, and with the right people as the key ingredients. I then told

Lief I had not yet seen Trunk, who had invited me, and asked him to point him out.

Lief found Trunk sitting on the back porch, made the introductions, and then made himself scarce. It was cold on the porch, so we moved our conversation inside. While standing in the kitchen, Trunk happened to hear one of his friends talking about the success of another friend. Instead of adding a positive remark, Trunk added negative comments. He seemed hell-bent on bashing people who made too much money and understood how to make the best of their employment opportunities; none of this had happened to him. It reminded me of the "poor woe-is-me" syndrome. I added my two cents and left the conversation on a dollar note. I was happy some people were experiencing the good life financially. My life was good too. I may not have acquired financial wealth but my life is rich with family, friends, and personal and professional relationships. I may not have a lot of money in my pockets but I have many hearts on my sleeve. For me, every day is Valentine's Day.

Space was what I needed at this moment, so I moved back into the living room to chat with Lief. A little later, I decided to give Trunk another try and once again found him on the back porch. This time, we actually had a conversation about friends and found out we had some in common. Trunk seemed nicer when we were talking one-on-one. Talking and drinking led to getting drunk. I did not want to lose my buzz, so drunk led to drunker for the both of us.

At some point in the laughter, Trunk asked if I would like to come over to his house for a while. I normally did not do this but it was one of those "Oh well, what the hell" kind of decisions. His house was down the block across from the Crack o' Dawn restaurant, and I still had my pocket knife in my pants. If he came after me with handcuffs, whips, or chains, I'd be able to cut myself free when he went to the bathroom for a potty break.

Trunk was totally embarrassed when we entered his place, the home that Uncle built. He had acquired his residence (or the "home is a man's castle") as a deceased relative's hand-me-down. The place was a mess. Trunk was a fixer-upper of sorts, and parts of other men's junk, that became his "treasures," were strewn all over the hardwood floor. Due to the wood, it was easy to kick things and make them scatter. I thought this may have been his idea of interior decorating. It reminded me of the 1970s comedy hit *Sanford and Son* with Redd Foxx as the junk man and the keeper of the treasures (or trash). Trunk and Sanford would have made great pals. Neither one would get rid of anything and could create the home that trash built. I think Jack the Hammer could complete this picture perfectly.

The best thing about Trunk's place was his dog, Bark. This may seem like a far-fetched name for a dog, but Bark was notorious for his deep bark and far-fetching talent for catching balls. I love dogs, and Bark was adorable. Trunk did an excellent job as a personal trainer with him, since he was friendly, not in the overbearing manner, but exuding a genuine sense of affection complemented with manners.

Once the playing with Bark was over, in addition to the tour of "a man's home is his castle," we decided to plop ourselves down on the couch. Trunk began kissing me, and a necking fest took place. For a confirmed bachelor, Trunk was a great kisser; it was just kissing, plain good old kissing with no Frenchmen invited. My thoughts were with regard to kissing as the limit. We both knew a few of the same people, and I was not on vacation in a foreign country. Also, Trunk was a confirmed bachelor, and this needed to be thoroughly investigated before I ended up with another package of frozen peas and carrots.

The kissing continued, we did a little chatting, petted Bark, and then out of the mouth of the confirmed bachelor came, "I like oral ..." and I can tell you the rest of the sentence did not involve hygiene. I was a little shocked, but mostly I just wanted to laugh out loud. Who said this to a gal at the first meeting, which wasn't even a date? Talk about being blunt and to the point. Also, it wasn't like we were in Phase Two and actually being intimate; there was no prerequisite anything to have allowed this to come from his lips. I certainly was not going to give him a reason for using my lips for oral hygiene. I didn't want my dentist suggesting two new toothbrushes at my next dental check-up. I can just hear the dental hygienist saying, "Naughty, naughty, I see we haven't been taking care of our mouth lately, and it appears you have had way too much oral activity."

Since I was drunk, I just thought Trunk was plain, as in *Sarah Plain and Tall* stupid, and also drunk. No wonder he didn't have a girlfriend (I didn't think he had a girlfriend but could be wrong). I wondered if this was his pick-up line and in his bachelor mind the words made him a real man. I should have asked him if he knew Oxy, since the two of them were about their manhood and can't just come out and say the word penis.

Of course, I told him oral sex was not a part of tonight's agenda and I would rather pet Bark than have Trunk expect me to fondle him. I knew this would also cross the line with Chelsea Handler, because she had a similar situation and oral sex was a nonnegotiable on the first date. If Chelsea said this was not okay, then it was definitely not the right thing to do at a first meeting of drunken minds, which could become *Dangerous Minds*. Stupid is as stupid does, and this phase of getting to know each other was more than over. Even Forrest Gump has enough sense to know when to go home and what not to tell his mama.

Trunk gave me his business card with his home phone number so we could stay in touch. I looked at the back side to see if he had a disclaimer about oral sex. No disclaimer or "want ad," so I chalked up this experience with his fascination for one-liners. Henny Youngman was much more successful with this approach. I certainly don't remember any oral sex one-liners. "Take my wife, please" received much more laughter. "Take my wife, please, because she is not into oral sex," would have Ed Sullivan cutting him off at the waist, much like what he did with Elvis Presley and his "hunka hunka burning love" and shaking hips.

I took the business card and in return gave him my phone number on one of the scraps of paper littered on the floor. Feeling a slap across the back of my head, I turned around and saw *Sarah Plain and Tall* stupid frowning at me. Sarah usually shows up when I am in the excessive party mode, but due to my more frequent bouts of stupidity and penchant for Carp, she has become less discretionary and visits more regularly. Seeking Dolly Lama's advice with regard to Sarah's visits became a mental hash mark on my forehead as an agenda item during my next long run past the bed and breakfast.

I must have been friends with Johnny Cash in a former life, since next I asked Trunk to walk the line with me to my car. I was sure if I stayed any longer I would walk the line straight to Folsom Prison for chopping off his oral sex. Also, even though I had sobered up quite a bit, I still might blow a 0.75, which in math rounds off to a 0.8, and end up without a "Get-Out-of-Jail-Free" card and spend the night enjoying spaghetti with the good, the bad, and the ugly. How can all this possibly happen to a woman who has gone through menopause?

It was after two in the morning, I was not in the safest part of town, the bars were closed, and many of the drunks were congregating across the street and waiting for breakfast at the Crack o' Dawn. There were no kisses at the car door, we barely said good-bye, and I drove away with the radio blaring Quiet Riot: "Bang your head, wake the dead." Trunk did not call to see if I made it home safely or to inquire if I had spent the night in jail awaiting my guest appearance on *America's Most Wanted* for driving on the fumes of alcohol. I had no intention of calling him.

Two days later, I visited Dolly Lama during my morning run. I told her about my oral night and frequent *Sarah Plain and Tall* stupid visits. She was silent for longer than usual, and when she finally opened her mouth, out came something I did not expect to hear. She bleated loudly she had heard much stranger stories with regard to sheep and left it at that; I understood.

Trunk called a few days later to make sure I didn't forget him, which I already had. I felt like telling him I had spent the last couple of days at Sex Anonymous trying to erase the mental image of him and oral sex. Anyway, he asked if I would like to go out to dinner on the weekend. More stupid continued, and I said yes.

The weekend arrived, and Trunk called to tell me he had to cancel our dinner date due to a surprise visit from several of his college friends. This sounded like a little crock but not a big crock, so I settled for the fondue pot excuse. He continued with excessive chatter about the warm weather for the upcoming week and he has been dying to get his Indian chopper out for a ride. Well, I did not know he had an Indian chopper and said so. Trunk told me he had seven choppers. Well, you have got to be kidding me. Seven Choppers and no women; well, this says a lot. I asked him why so many bikes. He explained they were all in parts in his basement, and he was in his fixer-upper mode.

Well, this certainly made sense. His basement must resemble his living room. Why was I not surprised? I should conference-call Big Boob and see if he was interested in writing more course work including solving math problems with motorcycle parts. What is it with guys and parts? Don't they understand that it is the whole and not the parts that is the desired outcome for all things in life?

It seemed the fondue pot was cracking and I needed to get the crock pot out of the cupboard to hold all the crap I was being fed. As a stew, the possibilities were bachelor pea casserole, bachelor carrot surprise, and bachelor corn à la poop. Liar is a coarse word, so I simmered down and asked Trunk how it was possible for him to drive to my house with his Indian chopper when all the parts are strewn all over the basement floor. He assured me one bike would be in operating condition before the weekend.

I had another thought that never formulated into a question. How on earth do you drive an Indian chopper out of a basement? I didn't remember seeing a chopper ramp. I knew Bark spent time in the backyard, so how could there be a ramp in his space? As a math person, none of this was adding up, but I said fine. What is a four-letter word starting with the letter *F*? Fine. For reasons I do not know, I was not in the Focker mode, nor had I reached my zenith with the F-bomb.

Another phone call a few days later had Trunk telling me the transformer leading to his house and several others was struck by a bolt of lighting and he once again had to cancel our date. He was without electrical power. I knew this was probably not a big crock pot, since I too was without power from the same storm, but after all the other oral communications, this story made me think we were getting closer to more crocks and they all fit in the same pot. How in the poop did this happen to me? I knew it was all Sarah's fault, or maybe it was a side effect of the night I spent with Jamie Foxx, which gives me creative license to blame it on the al-al-al-alcohol.

The weekend arrived and another phone call from Trunk and his progress with the Indian chopper. He explained a lot of technical crap, and I just didn't give a crap. I listened with half an ear. I was Trunked out. I never heard from or saw him again.

Summation: There is no Epilogue to this short story and a summation seems more fitting. Trunk, as a confirmed bachelor, had not acquired the skill set of how to actually follow through on a date, thus my willingness to be a Pollyanna with visits from *Sarah Plain and Tall* stupid. I had to admit I was initially disappointed, because he seemed to really have a lot going for him. He was easy to talk with, seemed genuinely interested in me, was a great kisser, and was a pet owner. I am over my disappointment, but there is a part of me hoping that Trunk finds a mate for Bark. With this in mind, there may be some little trees in the future, and what better way to bless the world than planting seedlings with one of the nicest dogs I ever met.

> *A single man has not nearly the value he would have*
> *in a state of union. He is an incomplete animal.*
> *He resembles the odd half of a pair of scissors.*
>
> —*Benjamin Franklin*

Part V
Higher Education

Education is the ability to meet life's situations.

—Dr. John G. Hibben

Past and Present Fishing

Online e-mailing with a
Fella I should know
I look and I look
And I still don't know.

Hints from his end
Telling me about my favorite beat
And pharmacy ice cream sugary treats
But still not knowing on this end.

Streets and avenues hint
Of this I know
My goodness gracious
How can this be so?

After so much time
Thirty years has been spent
You still look the same
And so do you I relent.

Childhood friends
Can older companions be?
It sort of feels fine
But sort of cannot be.

For in the end
To acknowledge the past
Puts smiles on our faces
But not lovers, we remain friends.

Al Minus the Family

Adventure One

Incoming Carp E-mail: I am of the big, large economy-size found in the bulk food section, tall and definitely good looking. I am interested in tattoos, bus tokens, strange destination travel vouchers, and Samaritan acts.

My philosophy of dating is to just fart right away.

—Jenny McCarthy

Introduction: After the Carp-foolery involving and progressing through a couple of bachelors, I decided my skill set worthy of a bachelor's degree and moved onto real "higher education," which is the master of arts. With passing on all past Carp, my grade book was full and time to move on to either finding the "Big One" or staying single and just having a bunch of boyfriends, since there weren't any adult males.

The Novella: It was Sunday morning and I was looking at a Fish who looked familiar but did not look familiar. I couldn't seem to put the face with a place of reference, so I sent a short note and asked him to read my bio and respond if interested. Immediately, I received a reply.

Mr. Somewhat Familiar responded and said I, too, looked familiar and he knew me from our pasts. I stared and stared and stared some more and replied I give up and have no clue as to who he is. He decided to give me three hints. The hints focused on an underground crosswalk from the local library and bakery, a big sand hill we used to jump off at a brick factory, and a cemetery where the high school kids congregated for make-out sessions. The last clue was the best clue since this fella seemed attracted to morbidity.

Taking another look at the photo, I recognized my childhood friend Al. Al is not his name but since he liked to play games with online anonymity, Al seemed like a perfect fit. Once again, I found it fondue pot strange I had met a Woodcock who didn't dance, Jack who didn't swim but liked the water, No Shame who loved to dine but didn't have any money, and now Al, who was on a dating site and wanted to remain anonymous. Go figure (or better yet, go figure not).

With the exchange of e-mails, Al told me he had the bad habit known as the smoke and choke and had tried to quit several times with no success. I told him I drank gallons of wine and had not tried to quit with every bit of success. So the summation was we now had a smoker and a drinker on different sides of the online fishing pond. I was not thinking of Al in a "lover" sense, and the "not drinking" meant we could never both wake up with our faces flat on the pillow. There was just something about not mixing with nondrinkers. They never understand the incessant laughing, the loss of inhibitions, and the desire to sing karaoke.

He continued with telling me he had been single for almost twenty years and enjoyed dating but had not yet met Ms. What I Am Looking For. He shared a few war stories and I just listened, believing kissing and telling was not appropriate. I was able to offer some small talk, mentioning that the men in my age dating group were a sorry bunch. They all looked like they had appeared on *Cops* and *America's Most Wanted*. Al said, "What about me? Do I fit in those categories?"

I said, "No, and the reason is why I wrote you the short note. I didn't respond to the others because I had no desire spending time with fellas whose interests included eating Froot Loops at the county jail."

Al continued by telling me he had a fifty-foot yacht at a marina on Lake Mackerela and would love to do a summer day trip when the weather was nice. Since it was early spring, I told him fine and in the near future we would have a "Hot Time in the Summertime" and listen to Sly and the Family Stone from the 1960s. Al was a nut about the music of the early '60s, not Led Zeppelin, Steppenwolf, and other acid trippers of the day.

I, on the other hand, loved all music, especially if it involved banging my head and raising the dead and other lyrics of exponential awareness by Quiet Riot. Judas Priest and "Living after Midnight" was also one of my favorites. I digress with regard to Judas Priest from my pay it backwards with Aqua Boy and the origin of their group's name. My mother used to say, "Judas Priest," when I was younger as a form of swearing instead of staying, "You little Focker." I heard many Polish women say this to their children. Of course, the Polish blamed it on the Ukrainians, who were known as lesser than the Poles. Either way, I knew I was in trouble when my mom was accompanied with Judas Priest. What happened next was a visit to the church confessional, and it had not even been two weeks since my last visit. I am sure the priest, who was not named Judas, was getting impatient listening to me tell him I had been a little Focker about fifty-six times. I know I never kept track but fifty-six sounded like a reasonable number of Fockers for a seven-year-old girl.

It was now July, and my Ya Ya sister from the land of nothing decided she had seen enough corn and made plans to visit me for a week. I hadn't seen Ya Ya since my carpet-cleaning days, and a gal vacation sounded fabulous. Ya Ya loved fishing, and so this week would be about finding Fish. I told her about Al and his big yacht on Lake Mackerela and swimming with various species of prey. The land of corn only had irrigation and it had been a long time since she had done more with water other than running through drops in a field.

So, in the air, on the ground, hugging, luggage thrown in the bedroom, and we were on our way to Al's house, the house that Sister built. Al lived with his sister and was deeply indebted to her since she allowed him to dwell for free. I, too, live for free but still had to pay homeowner's insurance and taxes twice a year.

Since I hadn't seen Al in forever, I did not realize he was a tattoo man. Ya Ya and I were in shock with the two unsightly tattoos of a different woman on each of his forearms. He also sported more hair than an orangutan with a shaved butt. I told Ya Ya the tattoos must be of each of his previous wives, and he couldn't help the amount of hair. She commented there would be no plans in the working with her as the third tattoo or to swing from trees since she was more comfortable on the ground with lesser haired species. Regardless, he was offering his time and his yacht, so smiles were in order and comments were on hold. A gift of time is a gift of a lifetime.

Arriving at the lake put a smile on everyone's face. It was a beautiful day and once on the water, everyone loosened up. Later in the afternoon, we docked the boat and drove back to Al's house and said our good-byes. It was a great day and Ya Ya said, "*Uno mas no mas.*" Al was just too big, hairy, and tattooed. She returned to the land of nothing to look at corn, run through irrigation sprinklers, and once again remain single.

Actually, being single is not a bad concept, and I had grown quite fond of the status. No drama, come and go as I please, no worry if the Carp is allergic to cats, eating pizza from the center of the pie, and online shopping are worth shopping around for the right Mr. Right. If Jennifer Anniston can remain single, and I do consider her a gal with good values and judgment, then there is nothing wrong with any of us lesser mortals staying single. I'll bet her dad didn't chase her around the house with a litany of Judas Priests for behaving like a little Focker.

For the next few months, Al and I continued our platonic relationship since we were sick and tired of looking for Mr. and Mrs. Right gone wrong. He introduced me to his good friends, Chuck and Luck, and the four of us shared dinners and conversation to the point of entertaining a boating day. Sadly, the day was not a fair weather day, and we decided to cut short the time on the water and lengthen the time together with dinner and drinks.

We picked a trendy place near the waterfront. It was pricey, and since Al does not drink, I told him I would pay for my wine, and if he wanted to split the bill, this was fine too. Al would not hear of this so it was his lead and his tab. I do not remember what I ordered but do remember what I drank. I had a glass of wine, and I am sure it was white. I did not get drunk and stupid. This happened later after I met up with *Sarah Plain and Tall*.

After dinner, Al was looking at the tab and in his wallet, and this made me feel uncomfortable. Regardless, Al looked, and I must say "looked" because I was looking at his eyes a little worried about the total tab. I should have asked him if he wore glasses. I did not go overboard with my meal and one drink. The meal tabs were paid, and

145

we all decided to drive into the city to a karaoke bar and have a few more drinks to complete the night. Singing and maybe seeing the Bong Sisters once again was now on the agenda.

Chuck, Luck, and I were in rare form once we entered the karaoke bar known as the Singing Banshees. The drinks were cheap and the entertainment was free. Chuck, Luck, and I ordered multiple drinks and began experimenting on how many different ways we can laugh dependent upon the liquid. Wine brought laughs with snorts, beer brought laughs with belches and farts, and hard liquor made us all laugh quicker. We had now met *Sarah Plain and Tall* stupid, and since she didn't have any plans, she said she would spend the rest of the evening helping us get hammered. My friend Tony told me "hammered" sounds less offensive than getting drop dead drunk (or *borracho* when referenced by Hispanics) and should always be used when the recreation includes excessive alcohol accompanied with uncontrollable laughter .

Chuck and Luck loved to sing and sang well. I, on the other hand, do more dancing and pass it off as singing. I completely forgot about Al, who ordered multiple Cokes and did not sing. At one point, I looked at him and thought, "I cannot do this." What a sorry looking, moping face. Or maybe he was thinking the same thing about the three of us and Sarah, whom we picked up and asked to tag-a-long; not to be confused with my Maui friend Tag-a-Long. Regardless, there was no meeting of the minds when drinking and singing were on one side of the fishing pond and Coke and dour mood was on the other. The night ended, Al went back to his boat, Chuck and Luck ducked down the alley with Sally, and I made the short drive home to sleep with my cats, which don't smoke cigarettes or mix dour with dough and resemble a slice of stale bread.

> *If you don't drink, then all of your stories suck*
> *and end with, 'And then I got home.'*
>
> —*Jim Jefferies*

Al and the Family

Adventure Two

> *As I look back over my life, before I had any real identity,*
> *I was a traveler. I grew up an army brat, a runaway, an*
> *activist, and a musician. All my life I've been traveling.*
>
> —*Michelle Shocked*

A year later, I bumped into Al in a professional building that housed technology and a few restrooms. I had an unplanned pee and thus the unplanned meeting. Since a year had passed, there was enough time for us to be separated and to start anew. I had no idea why I was entertaining thoughts of anew since we both knew and understood Al smoked and I drank. Waking up with my face flat on the pillow, thinking I can't believe I am alive and here for another day, is a spiritual moment everyone should experience more than once in their lifetime. A flat face is the result of an inflated night.

Al and I were now on round two of trying, and the operative word is trying since I was a few degrees cooler than lukewarm, to see if there may be some chemistry. I did not take chemistry in high school and was relying on physics. For me, it was about the science of a man and a woman and the equal in an equation as to a fit physically and intimately. Regardless, we decided to meet for dinner on the following Friday at a restaurant of my choice. I chose Flapper Fish since the Friday fish special comes with two complimentary glasses of white wine, but no

Sarah Plain and Tall stupid. I would have to pay for the third drink in order for her to show up.

Friday arrived and I was early and Al was late. Forty-five minutes later, Al entered and apologized and said he didn't *feel* tardy. Maybe he thought this was funny since he considered himself *Hot for Teacher*. I was not amused since David Lee Roth had gone to seed, and even a ripened kumquat looked better.

Al continued with an explanation regarding his older sister, who owned the house he lived in, which I already knew. What I did not know was Sister was·seventy years old and instigated trying circumstances as a normal daily occurrence. Al had to save the day just about every day. In his next breath, Al told me Sister left the house, lost her way, and then found her way to Cash in Your Coins in order to get cash for her accumulated bus tokens. She was obsessed with wandering, cashing in tokens, and traveling to exotic places. Sister gave Al a hard time since he foiled her plans to board a bus to Michigan's Adventures. The park had just installed a new water slide and the age limit was seventy-one. I told Al I would be excited too, but bingo placed higher on my list of the one thousand things I planned to do before I died. With this said, we ordered dinner and continued our conversation with regard to our lives with amusing misfits. In paying the tab, Al did not look into his wallet with despair, and we parted on a good note.

A week later, another dinner plan and Sister boarded a plane to Beijing to scale the Great Wall with her friends the Grayed Hairs, which are archenemies of the Red Hats. Sister would never don a red hat to cover her gray hair. Once again, Al told me he had to make an interception before Sister did something he would regret. I thought it would be the regret of Sister but Al explained she never regrets but forgets. Everything she did got *Lost in Space* much like the TV series from the late 1960s. For all he knew, she may be painting the Grand Dame's red hat bright fuchsia. Sister certainly seemed feisty, and I was thinking of becoming her gal friend. I told him we could cancel and make this dinner on a different date. He said, "No, Sister never left the ground and I will only be about an hour late."

I said, "Fine, I have a magazine and may be drunk by the time you arrive."

He said, "Fine, I would not expect it any other way."

I behaved and read my magazine with only one glass of wine. Al once again arrived late, saying, "I don't feel tardy," and told me he left Sister in the custody of Big Brother as a safety measure since she seemed to need siblings. We ordered and ate dinner. Al was a gentleman, paying the tab, and we decided to meet the following Friday for a church-sponsored gambling night, which he supported.

Friday arrived and we decided to meet first for dinner before the gambling began. Sister once again got loose with her full jar of bus tokens and was now on her way to Cedar Point Amusement Park in Sandusky, Ohio. Al said his nephew, named Nephew, intercepted Sister at the bus stop in Detroit and was driving her home. He wanted to wait until Nephew and Sister arrived safely. I told Al I had a magazine and it was happy hour, so I was fine. I had no problem with being happy.

Al arrived and Sister and Nephew were safe at Big Brother's. He looked distressed and this was totally understandable. After dinner, Al looked into his wallet at his stash of cash and told me he was short or could not make change (I don't remember). I, on the other hand, rarely have cash since I am a card-carrying gal. Fortunately, for once in my life, I had a little of the paper wonder stuff and gave Al twenty dollars and tip money.

My spirit needed a lot of lifting at this point, since happy hour was definitely over and Al was exhausting me with his math patterns and problem solving with Sister, who was "A Little Runaway" and not even related to Jon Bon Jovi. I was not sure she even traveled in pants. I dismissed all of this when we arrived at the church casino. Wine, fun, and money were on my mind, and in that order.

Al and I both signed in and received a gaming credit card for accrued monies, and I also received an additional fifty dollars of funny money since this was my first time to attend such an event. As a gesture of goodwill, Al also received fifty dollars of funny money since he was accompanied by a first-timer. Al had a grocery bag full of Sister's quarters and was on the stash side of possible winnings. I, on the other hand, had fifty dollars of funny money and promised myself not to lose more than a total of seventy.

Al and I went to an aisle of slots and began with our funny money. I quickly lost mine and decided to gamble with a glass of wine from the nearest bar station. Before I left Al, he played his funny money and won eight hundred dollars. He smiled and pointed at his winnings. I was happy for him and decided to wait a minute to see if he was able to add more dollars. The numbers went up and down, and he basically walked away with $795. He told me to go get my wine and he would meet me in another aisle. I asked what aisle. He told me to just look for the winner. I was not smiling now since I did not bring my traveling pants and did not plan to follow him and his pointing finger.

I sat at the bar station and chatted with a couple of gals who were two drinks ahead of me and now had the gift of gab. I chatted longer than I planned, but who plans when drinking is the top agenda line item? We spent about half an hour together and then the gals decided to spend the rest of their money and maybe become winners. I, on the other hand, reluctantly went to look for the "winner." I found him with his wad of winnings stuffed in the grocery bag with Sister's quarters and looking like he should be friends with Jed Clampet and *The Beverly Hillbillies.*

Al continued to play slots, continued to win, and continued to point his finger at the dollar amounts. I just wanted to take his finger and pull it to see if it farted. The night continued and in the end I think I broke about even. I was not about counting peas and carrots and am better at ballpark frank figures.

Al won a lot of money, did not share any of his money, and made the excuse Sister's bag is worth a nickel at the grocery store and it was a better idea if he returned her stash. Sister may want to make a quick getaway to Madison, Wisconsin's Lake Wingra since it is Carp-free. It seemed funny, strange that Al related a possible Sister adventure focusing on a Carp-free environment. Maybe females with traveling pants are just as concerned with bottom feeders as with those of us who wear jeggings and tights with tunic tops.

At the end of the evening, the big prize drawing was held, which we both bought tickets for. You guessed it; Al won and it was a win with choices. The choices were a trip for one to Las Vegas to see Ted Nugent in his Fred Bear gear or a weekend stay at Mackinaw Island for two. Al picked the trip to Vegas, and he doesn't even fish or hunt. What on earth did he have in common with Ted Nugent? Al drove me back to my car at the restaurant and we parted for the evening.

During my drive home, I assessed the night and did some mental math problem solving. I asked myself the important questions, which will be the decision makers of another night with Al. Was Al selfish? He can be, since he won a ton of money and did not even give me a quarter to play with at the slot next to him. Yes, I knew we were using gaming cards but he cashed in his card several times and did not even give me a quarter, not even one from Sister's grocery bag. I would have given him at least a dollar. I would have probably given the big Focker a hundred dollars, and I definitely would have picked the trip to Mackinaw Island to share since we spent this time together. I certainly would not have invited Ted Nugent, who is always packed for bear. The compulsory looks in his wallet to assess his cash was nothing compared to how this night evolved. Now that I think about it, maybe I was just his escort. For this, I definitely should have been paid at least a hundred dollars and given the opportunity to pull his finger to get rid of the bad gas trapped in the seat of his pants.

Previous to this weekend fiasco, we had agreed to another dinner date with Chuck and Luck. I decided to do the wrong thing and asked a girlfriend for advice since I still hadn't acquired a will with my spine. She got me even more riled up than I was in the first place, and in the second place made me go to the computer and write Al a Dear Al and the Family letter, without even a breather from my complaints.

The e-mail noted all my frustrations, and I concluded I just couldn't be the last item on his grocery list. I was worth more than a nickel grocery bag, had my own pair of traveling pants known as jeggings, did not save quarters due to an addiction to online shopping, and did not have the time to be obsessed with regard to *Men Behaving Badly*. Mostly, I did not like what the past experiences had done to my behavior and attitude. I had become an old goat and felt that keeping company with Dolly Lama may be a better choice.

Al returned my e-mail and stated he was in shock. He assumed we had a great time since he thought I was happy with breaking even with my money, did not ask him to spend the nickel for the grocery bag with Sister's stash, and loved reading magazines while waiting for him. *Oh Brother, Where Art Thou* was all I can think. I didn't even respond. I had nothing to say.

I wished this could have ended differently but it didn't. It was difficult for me not to beat myself up when things went awry, and this experience was no exception. In fact, it is still bothersome today. Yes, I was awful but we were awful together. Forrest Gump and his peas and carrots could have figured this one out before the bag of frozen vegetables defrosted in the microwave.

Epilogue: After more than a year of misery to an unwanted attraction, I once again consulted Dolly on my run past the bed and breakfast. She asked me if it was possible if Al and I could just remain friends. I told her not a fart on this earth was big enough to move me in the direction of trying to establish whatever for the third time. It was just *Sarah Plain and Tall* stupid. As a math person and believer in patterns, the scenario would be repeated, and we as people were difficult to change. Al would not change, and this was good for him. I would change if need be, and this would be good for me. In the meantime, I would give people quarters and smile when I saw Dolly on my daily run. I didn't have to pull her ear to hear her fart. She is a real lama and also a real lady who knows not to mingle with sheep. I will try to model her behavior in that I should not mingle with Carp. The operative word is "try" since the understanding of Carp is not a true science and confuses me with mutants.

Everyone is a friend, until they prove otherwise.

—sent by Steve

I'm a Rich Man, but I've Gone Too Far

I am a rich man with condos
In cities including San Diego
Close to the water
where property is prime.
I can go swimming in the ocean
just a walk down two blocks.
I can run and bike,
eat fine food, drink wine, and the like.

I am a rich man with connections,
big corporations, and private jets.
Fine clothes, fine friends, fine money with
weekend safaris, jaunts, and visits to inner continents.
Hunting wildebeests in Africa, fly fishing in Montana,
and singing with the Mariachi bands
In southern Oaxaca.

I am a rich man and have dated many gals
Younger ones, older ones, blonde haired and brunettes.
Out of their comfort zone
of these I desire
Rich men, older men, I am the master and squire.

I am a rich man and tight with my dollars.
For in being frugal, I can shower myself with powers.
I have endless funds to tell you about.
Across from you I sit and shout.
My accomplishments are many
And I cannot get enough
of being a rich man with powers and stuff.

You are a rich man, of this I know.
Across from you I sit, not talking
and listening to the show.
Grandeur, elegance, and splendor you speak

And from me not so much as a sigh or a peep
for you are a rich man with condos and women who do not sleep.

You are a rich man, of this I know
I have listened to all
And this I know
While sitting here you stick me with my bill
of ten dollars for a salad with honey and dill.

And this mantra from a rich man of this I know
who has all that he needs and is a glow.
But to not spend ten dollars on a gal who loves salad
Is not a part of his future adage
For in his conjecture
Little does he know
That I, too, am a rich gal in all that I know
Family, friends, and love at a squeeze
with smiles, laughs, and generosity.

For the rich man is really poor at heart
He doesn't understand what is truly his part
For the rich man who has all of his needs
Misses what is richest of what he should be
For it is with his riches he chooses to fall
By choosing not to surround himself
with those who are the richest of all.

Conclusion

In thinking of my past experiences with dating, I have learned it is a challenging process, much like trying to catch a "keeper" bass or musky. What defines a keeper with the human species is much more complicated than just defining length. We are all very complicated people regardless of gender, and the older we get, the more cumbersome we may become. Values, beliefs, how much one is willing to compromise, and one's past are a part of every date, and these can either make or break the fishing rod.

In the meantime, I will think about the Carp who are already staring at me from the bottom of my new bucket. Included are Baked Alaska, Napoleon Dynomite, Ferris Wheel Carnie, Kielbasa and Floppy just to mention a few. One would think that after finishing a book full of Carp foolery I would be exhausted, but this is not the case. When beginning my journey, I skipped preschool and kindergarten, and therefore the powers that be told me I did not qualify for a graduate degree. I am not bothered with the thought of furthering my fishing education since I really enjoy school and do not mind being a professional student. I never thought that when I grew up and people asked me what I did for a living that the answer would be I swim with Carp.

In closing, my thoughts are best stated in the lyrics by the rock group U2: "I still haven't found what I'm looking for." Mindful, I will continue to fish. I have always considered myself a Pollyanna in the sense that I am hopeful. I am hopeful there is a Fish who will catch and keep my heart. My next fishing date may be in an aisle in a grocery store. I also have thoughts of visiting Menards and Lowe's since men seem fixated with nuts and rods, or maybe it is nuts and bolts.

> *In every species of fish I've angled for, it is the ones that have got away that thrill me the most, the ones that keep fresh in my memory. So I say it is good to lose fish. If we didn't, much of the thrill of angling would be gone.*
>
> —*Ray Bergman*

Part VI
Quotables for a Dollar: My
Life's in Jeopardy, Baby

Cindy Lucy and Carp

Cindy Lucy: *Why did I bother to shave my legs? This Carp has more hair sprouting out of the top of his shirt collar, the inside of his nose, and his ears than I have on my entire body. I wonder if first dates should come with a razor.*

Cindy Lucy: *Does your age match your waistline? Let's see, you are sixty-five years old and, yes, you do have a sixty-five-inch waist. No wonder you wear flip-flops to dinner.*

Carp: *I'm sorry, Cindy Lucy, but there just isn't any chemistry between us.*
Cindy Lucy: *Well, if you weren't bouncing around in your seat as if you forgot your medication, this might have added at least the "c" in chemistry to our fishing.*

Cindy Lucy: *Did you confuse sex with chemistry? Are first dates about sex and then you decide whether there is chemistry?*

Carp: *I am busy every day except Sunday. How does Sunday at 3:00 p.m. work for you?*
Cindy Lucy: *Bradley Cooper told me that's not gonna happen. I'll be recovering from a hangover. Liquid dinner with someone else was much more enjoyable.*

Cindy Lucy

Cindy Lucy: *How come your picture with your bio shows you thirty years younger and fifty pounds lighter? Is that your baby picture you have on file?*

Cindy Lucy: *Nice car.*
Carp: *This is not my car. I borrowed it from a friend who promised I could catch a gal if I drove it.*
Cindy Lucy: *Well, keep on driving because Carp like you are known as drive-bys and good-byes.*

Carp: *I see you are a runner. Don't ask me to run.*
Cindy Lucy: *I am not asking you to run, and I am not asking you to walk either. These are not pick-up lines. They are called you dropped the ball and I kicked.*

Carp: *My ex-wife lives in the beautiful house next door, and I live in this shack. I decided to live next door so I could see what I once had.*
Cindy Lucy: *Well, your future doesn't look bright so you better take off your shades.*

Carp: *I love reading books even though I have not read one in the past twenty years. Oh, yes, does bathroom reading count?*

Carp: *Cindy Lucy, you have such ugly feet, hide them.*
Cindy Lucy: *Well, don't look at them.*

Cindy Lucy: *Men and Pavlov's dog are related. Both of them are trained to salivate.*
Carp: *Who's Pavlov? Is he a member of the rock group Kiss?*

Carp: *Thanks for putting up with me.*
Cindy Lucy: *Yes, thanks to you, too, for putting up with yourself.*

Cindy Lucy: *If you want to get screwed, you better not screw it up.*
Carp: *Does that mean I can still bring along my ex-wives and children and let them live next door?*

Carp: *Take your glasses off so I can see what you look like.*
Cindy Lucy: *Well then, you take off your pants so I can see what you look like.*

Cindy Lucy: *Carp generally seem to be unhappy and use me for therapy. It is easy to be objective, but as for giving advice, there isn't any, since each species is a separate being in itself with no baseline or variables for problem solving.*

Cindy Lucy: *Vanity has no affair except with itself.*

Cindy Lucy: *Blind ambition is better than no ambition.*